PLAYING FOR KEEPS

JOAN LOWERY NIXON

DELACORTE PRESS

Published by
Delacorte Press
an imprint of
Random House Children's Books
a division of Random House, Inc.
1540 Broadway
New York, New York 10036

Visit us on the Web! www.randomhouse.com/teens
Educators and librarians, for a variety of teaching tools, visit us at
www.randomhouse.com/teachers

Library of Congress Cataloging-in-Publication Data
Nixon, Joan Lowery.
Playing for keeps / Joan Lowery Nixon.
p.   cm.
Summary: On a Caribbean cruise, sixteen-year-old Rosie meets a
teenage Cuban baseball player seeking political asylum in the
United States and tries to help him escape a charge of murder.
ISBN 0-385-32759-5 (trade)   ISBN 0-385-90014-7 (lib. bdg.)
[1. Cruise ships—Fiction.   2. Refugees—Fiction.   3. Caribbean
Area—Fiction.   4. Mystery and detective stories.]   I. Title.

PZ7.N65 Pn 2001
[Fic]—dc21   00-065821

The text of this book is set in 11-point Trump Mediaeval.

Book design by Melissa Knight

Manufactured in the United States of America

August 2001

10 9 8 7 6 5 4 3 2 1

BVG

PLAYING FOR KEEPS

⟞PROLOGUE⟝

ENRIQUE HUDDLED IN THE BOTTOM OF THE SMALL BOAT, as Raúl had warned him to do.

Where is Raúl?

With only a thin cat's smile of a moon to break the heavy blackness of the night sky, it was difficult to see, and the water against the pier muffled the voices outside the nearby *cantina*.

Raúl? Where are you?

Could Raúl have been stopped by the *policía*? What if he'd been cornered and had babbled about the escape, and the *policía* were about to storm across the beach? Enrique's hands were sticky with sweat, and he wiped them down the sides of his khaki trousers. He knew what would happen. He'd be dragged from the boat and taken back to Havana.

1

Enrique's rapid heartbeat thudded in his ears. He'd been warned about the fate of those who had tried to flee Cuba and failed. Some were beaten, starved in prison ... In his own case he'd be branded a defector—as much a traitor to his country as if he'd deserted the military. The penalty for this crime against the state could be death.

Suddenly a large, dark mass loomed over the side of the boat, and Enrique choked noisily on his own fear.

"*¡Silencio!*" Raúl's whisper was more of a deep rumble. "Do you want everyone from the *cantina* to hear you?"

Enrique felt the boat being shoved from the dock. The motor caught, and the boat headed for the pass between the Camagüey islands.

Raising his head and squinting to make out Raúl's features in the darkness, Enrique asked, "Aren't you going to use lights?"

"I don't need lights," Raúl said.

"But how can you see to read your compass?"

"I don't need a compass. I know these waters, and they know me. They show me the way. I'm the best boatman in Cuba. That's why your uncle hired me to take you to Haiti."

"My *great*-uncle," Enrique corrected.

"*No importa.*" Raúl's chuckle was one of delight. "Eight thousand dollars makes me a very rich man," he said.

So that is what Uncle Martín had to pay.

2

Enrique wrapped his arms across his chest, rubbing his shoulders as if they were cold. This was only part of the price of freedom. How could he ever repay Uncle Martín?

The boat suddenly picked up speed, and Ricky sat upright, trying to discover what was happening without asking Raúl. The white beaches of Cayo Coco seemed to catch the thin light, reflecting it against the froth of breaking waves along the eastern shore. To the far north the lighted windows in a new hotel shone in a tidy grid, but before Enrique had time to think about what he had seen, the lights and the glowing sand had disappeared like a mirage.

The gentle waters of the bay changed to rough swells, and the little boat slapped the rises hard, sometimes plunging down and up again with a sickening jerking motion. Enrique clung to the sides of the boat, fighting the bile that rose in his throat. "Where are the life jackets?" he managed to ask.

Raúl laughed, this time making no attempt to be quiet. "No life jackets, no overhead. It seems that the star baseball player is not so good a sailor," he said.

Enrique didn't try to answer. He sucked in the cool air, feeling better as it stung his face.

He realized that Raúl didn't expect him to speak. Raúl seemed more interested in himself. "I watched you just last week when you stood on the pitcher's mound in the *Estadio Latinoamericano* and received a special award from Fidel Castro himself. You have a strong arm for one only seventeen years old."

"*No importa.*" Enrique tried not to listen, but Raúl went on.

"In his speech Fidel said many extravagant things about your future."

"*No importa,*" Enrique repeated.

Raúl's voice rose with exaggerated incredulity. "*¿No importa?* When everyone in the Cuban league knows both you and your record? When you pitch a shutout game for the Habana Leónes? When Fidel himself puts an arm about your shoulders and proclaims himself your special patron? How can that not matter?"

Enrique could only groan.

Raúl was silent for a few minutes. Then he said, "I know your grandmother. Sometimes when I am in Old Havana I pass your house in the late afternoon and see Beatriz on the front porch. Back and forth she rocks, always smoking a fat cigar. I wave, and she waves back. She and my father were among Fidel's young revolutionaries."

"I know," Enrique answered quickly, hoping it would stop Raúl from reminiscing. Much as he loved his stern grandmother, with her back as straight as the upright posts on a kitchen chair and her voice as sharp as the click of a knife on a plastic breadboard, he had heard Abuela Beatriz speak much too often about Fidel Castro's glorious rise to power.

Raúl broke into Enrique's thoughts. "My father often told me that back in the fifties, when Beatriz fought with Fidel's forces, she was as tall and strong as any man. She did not brag about her family's Spanish blood and their privileged life under the protection of the dictator Batista. She was proud to be Cuban. She followed Fidel's star then, and I hear she is still as loyal as ever."

"Yes. She is," Enrique answered.

Raúl's words curled with sly curiosity through the darkness. "So how does she feel about you deserting Cuba?"

"I am not deserting Cuba!" Enrique insisted. Tears burned his eyes as he thought of leaving the land he loved, the grandmother he loved, and especially the one he loved best, his great-aunt Ana.

Although Beatriz had become Enrique's guardian after his parents were killed in a factory fire, it was her sister—gentle Ana—who rocked Enrique and sang to him and played games with him and cooked his favorite fried bananas and sweet milk pudding as special treats. It was Ana who taught Enrique to throw a baseball when he was only five, and later took him to audition for the baseball academy, where he would get the best education on the island.

"You're like your great-uncle Martín," Ana

would say, and she'd tell Enrique about her brother-in-law who had played with the Cuban league until Fidel Castro's rise to power, when Martín had left Cuba for the United States and signed with the Cincinnati Reds.

"Martín left to find freedom," she'd say, and the words, as she spoke them, rang like small silver bells in Enrique's mind.

When Enrique grew older, able to see how Fidel's dictatorship was harming the Cuban people, he understood what Tía Ana's words really meant. They were more than words. They were more than silver bells. The search for freedom became the very heart of life.

It was Tía Ana who had worked with Uncle Martín to make arrangements to help Enrique escape to the United States, where he could ask for political asylum.

Eager to be through this first leg of his journey, Enrique asked, "How long until we reach Haiti?"

"Not long at all."

"What if we meet a patrol boat?"

"This little boat of mine is so low in the water it is missed by the patrol boats' radar," Raúl answered. "Also, it is faster than any patrol boat ever built. I have been chased more than once, but I easily outrun them. That is why people headed for Florida or the Bahamian islands hire me. That is why your uncle hired me. Never fear, young baseball star, your uncle's plan is not what I expected, but as he wishes, I will bring you to Haiti and to the people who will help you."

Enrique nodded; then, realizing that Raúl would not see that nod, he quietly said, *"Gracias."*

"No need for thanks," Raúl said, and laughed again—a laugh Enrique was beginning to hate. "The payment I was given is thanks enough."

Nothing more was said. Enrique, concerned only with his balance as the boat skimmed and slapped the surface of the ocean waters, lost all track of time. All he knew was that the night was still deep velvet—as Tía Ana used to call it—indicating the late night hours.

When they reached the island of Haiti, its shoreline was only a dark, forested blur to Enrique, but Raúl, unerring as a bat in the darkness, headed into a small inlet and docked at a rough pier.

"This way," called a soft voice in the darkness.

Obeying the words in English—a language Tía Ana had taught him well—Enrique struggled to his feet and climbed from the boat. He staggered a few steps as his body tried to adjust from the choppy waters to the stability of land, and then a hand gripped his arm.

A boy, a shadow in the dark night, looked up at Enrique, saying, "You be okay now. Come with me."

Enrique could hear Raúl's boat already moving back out to sea and realized he was alone in a strange land with a boy younger than himself—

thirteen? Fourteen?—whom he was entrusting with his life. "Who are you?" Enrique asked.

The boy hesitated, then said, "Call me Paki." Quickly he added, "Come along now. I give you a mat for a few hours' sleep. Then before light we go to Bonita Beach. Okay?"

Bonita Beach. Where I'll meet my uncle. "Okay," Enrique answered. He followed Paki past a line of beached canoes and rowboats to a cluster of makeshift houses in a clearing. Without turning on a light, the boy led Enrique inside one of the dwellings. Pointing to three dark bundles, one of which snored lightly, he whispered, "Don't step on my brothers."

Enrique was given a padded cotton mat, which he unrolled and spread across the only available floor space. He wearily lay on the mat, knowing he'd never be able to sleep. He was defying fate and creating deadly political enemies in the process. He was alienating his grandmother. He was parting forever from his beloved Tía Ana. He was headed for freedom in a strange country with a great-uncle he knew only from occasional letters. How could he sleep?

In spite of his worries, he must have. It seemed like only a few minutes later that he struggled to wake from fearful dreams and to pull away from the hands that gripped his shoulders in the darkness.

"Time to go now. Wake up!" Paki's voice was

urgent. He thrust a wide-brimmed straw hat at Enrique. "Wear this and come. We got no time to lose!"

Enrique hurried, stumbling after the boy. By the time they reached the inlet, a cluster of long, narrow canoes and rowboats crowded the water. Some of them were already filled and heading out to sea.

Someone called out to Paki, who jumped into the nearest canoe. He motioned to Enrique to follow.

As the boat shot forward, propelled by two men with paddles who sat fore and aft, Paki leaned toward Enrique. "Only way to get to Bonita Beach be by water," he said. "They take workers in early morning before ships come and pick them up at night, after ships leave. You got American dollar? You give to them. Okay?"

Enrique nodded. He had no Cuban pesos. They were worth nothing, even in Cuba, where the U.S. dollar was the currency of choice. Tía Ana had given him twenty U.S. dollar bills—the equivalent of a Cuban doctor's monthly salary—to use, if needed, before he made his connection with her brother-in-law, Martín Urbino.

Paki grinned. "And maybe a dollar for me, too. Okay?"

"Okay," Enrique said.

"You gimme now. I see they get paid."

Enrique reached into the inside pocket of his jeans and tugged out three one-dollar bills. He

passed them to Paki, who took them without
a word.

The canoe trailed the small boats ahead, hugging the thickly overgrown shoreline. Branches covered in broad, fleshy leaves tangled with rough
spikes of palm and fanlike leaves of sea grape, creating a tightly woven wall around the island. Enrique
couldn't imagine how anyone could penetrate it.

As they reached a peninsula with broad, sandy
beaches and widely spaced shade trees, Enrique
could see a man standing under a yellow lamp peering at a clipboard. Workers lined up before him, apparently giving their names, then trotted across the
packed sand to tend to the jobs they were hired
to do.

"Your white face be too different. Keep your head
down. Let your hat cover you," Paki whispered.

At one side of the area, between the curve of the
bay and the thick growth that covered a steep hill,
was a large open-sided pavilion surrounded by rows
of picnic tables and benches. Chatter and laughter
came from within the pavilion, where cooks must
already have been preparing lunch, and Enrique's
stomach clutched with hunger. When had he last
eaten? He couldn't remember.

Paki laid a hand on Enrique's shoulder and
whispered, "Be ready now. When we land you
move fast."

"Where should I go?"

"The old fort. I show you."

Their canoe shot around the beached ones, and the man with the clipboard raised his head. "Hey! Where you going?" he called.

"No room there, Mr. Dee," the man in the prow shouted back. He swung the canoe inland around a curve, beyond the director's line of sight.

"Now!" the boy said. He and the other men jumped from the canoe and waded the few steps to shore. Enrique followed.

While the men headed toward their check-in point, Paki scrambled up a low embankment, across a path through a thin scrub of forest, and through the broken doorway of what remained of a stone fort. Enrique stayed close behind.

"No one come here for a while," Paki said. "Just stay away from the trail so no one can see you."

"Where will I find my uncle?"

"No worry. He find you."

"When will he come?"

Paki pointed to the open expanse of water. "Ship be here eight-thirty. You see." He paused. "I go now."

Enrique nodded. "*Gracias.* Thank you."

Paki grinned again and was gone.

Enrique climbed into a sheltered corner among the roofless, broken walls of the small fort. He shivered, hugging his shoulders and rubbing his upper arms, but he couldn't rid himself of the fear that dampened the back of his neck and burned with a sour taste in his mouth.

Martín Urbino had passed his dreams and hopes to Enrique, but how could they possibly come true? As Fidel Castro's enemy, how could Enrique ever hope to escape?

I DIDN'T HAVE TIME TO THINK ABOUT MY ARGUMENT with Mom until Glory and I were in the air on the way to Miami. Then I had too much time.

Glory—Gloria Marstead—was my grandmother on my father's side. Mom sometimes complained that Glory had a salt-and-pepper attitude to go with her salt-and-pepper hair and liked getting her own way.

I have to agree. In spite of the fact that Grandpa made a great deal of money way back during the oil boom and invested it wisely before he died, Glory had continued to work as a successful attorney until she retired a year earlier.

"Defending people gives her an excuse to argue," I once heard Mom telling Dad. He thought what Mom said was funny. So did I. But Mom wasn't trying to be funny.

In the seat beside me Glory gave a light snore. I glanced at her, expecting her to wake up, but she continued to sleep peacefully. We'd had to catch a very early plane at the Midland-Odessa airport to connect with our flight out of Houston. I was tired, too, but there was no way I could sleep—not after the argument, which had never been resolved.

I couldn't help being excited about going with Glory on a week's cruise in the Caribbean, but deep down inside I had a sick feeling. I should have made peace with Mom before I left. I had wanted to, but I didn't know what to say or do, and Mom was so frozen in her own unhappiness I couldn't begin to reach her, even if I'd known how. I wasn't the only one at fault, I told myself. She had let me go without trying to break through that layer of ice.

The argument had started over a party I should never have gone to with a guy I hoped to totally forget.

"When you first saw what the party was like, Rose Ann, why didn't you ask your date to take you home?" Mom had asked.

I'd blushed and stared down at the scuffed toes of my sneakers. "Cam Daly wasn't . . . well, I found out that he only asked me to the party because a girl he likes was going to be there. Mom, he dumped me. I felt so stupid. I thought everybody was staring at me and thinking I was a real loser, so

I tried to act like I was having a good time celebrating spring break and didn't care."

Mom had just sighed and asked, "Rose Ann, you need to act with maturity. Aren't you ever going to stand up for what you believe in? Where is your courage?"

I'd groaned, knowing what was coming. "Are you going to bring up that time ages ago when Bobby Mac cheated from my test?"

"It wasn't ages ago. It was last September. You allowed him to see your paper and got caught doing it. And what about when Lou drove all of you in her family's car and you knew very well she didn't have her license yet. Why didn't you object?"

I'd slid another notch down on the sofa. "Do we have to go into all that again?"

"I'm trying to show you that it was the same situation with the party last night," Mom had said. "Be independent. Don't just go along with the crowd because of what somebody might think of you. Last night you abused my trust in you and the freedom I've given you."

"Trust? Mom, I made one little mistake. Can't you believe it was just a mistake? As for freedom—"

That was when Glory had arrived, making herself at home on the sofa. She'd heard all about the wild party. "There isn't anyone in west Texas who doesn't know every detail," Glory said. "Especially since someone had to call the police."

She shrugged as she added, "That boy you went

to the party with is not the kind you want to date. You want the right kind."

Mom broke in. Her voice was tight as she said, "It doesn't matter who was Rose Ann's date at the party. It only matters that she used very poor judgment."

Glory gave a more elaborate shrug. "Well, there you have it," she said. "Poor judgment. Certainly not a punishable offense. Rosie's suffered enough already. Why don't we talk about something I have in mind?"

Mom had been trying hard to hide her impatience. "Later, Glory," she'd said. "If you'll please excuse us, Rose Ann and I are not through with our family discussion. If you understood—"

"I understand one thing, Linda, which is while we're sitting here beating a dead horse, we're running out of time, and that's what we don't have much of. Let me borrow Rosie for a week."

Startled, Mom said, "But you won't be here. You're going on that Caribbean cruise with your bridge club."

That was when Glory told us she wanted to substitute me for her bridge club roommate, who was going to have foot surgery and couldn't make the cruise. "I'll take care of expenses. Rosie will be my guest."

"But you're leaving tomorrow morning."

Glory grinned. "Have you ever known me to be unable to do something I wanted to do? Don't worry. My travel agent's working on it already. All Rosie will need are her driver's license and birth certificate, T-shirts and shorts, and a couple of dresses she can wear to dinner. Toss in that cream-colored satin formal she wore to the winter prom. One dinner is formal dress."

I gasped, trying to take in what Glory was saying as she began giving Mom all the reasons why I should go with her, and explaining that I'd be perfectly safe on the ship while she was playing in the bridge tournament. My heart began to pound. A Caribbean cruise? Tomorrow?

I knew I shouldn't beg as I turned to Mom, but I couldn't help it. "I've never seen the ocean. I've never been out of Texas. I know you're angry with me, Mom, but please may I go?"

Mom had thought a moment, her face pale and tight. "I can't let you do this, Glory," she'd said.

"Who are you punishing, Linda?" Glory had bluntly asked. "Rosie or me?"

I could hear Mom's sharp intake of breath. Even though I really wanted to go on this cruise, I had to admit that Glory didn't always play fair.

It had been like this ever since Dad had died when I was fourteen, leaving a stack of medical bills. Glory had paid them and had even paid off the mortgage for the house we lived in. When Mom said my ballet lessons didn't fit the budget, they were paid for. There was our membership in a swim club Mom couldn't afford, new dresses for me from

Glory's favorite shops . . . the list was a long one. Mom protested, but Glory always won.

This time was no different. Mom looked at me with her eyes burning, then quickly turned her head and said to Glory, "I'll have her ready."

After Glory had left, Mom walked to the end of the room, staring out the windows overlooking the backyard. Her voice dropped, as if she were speaking to herself. "Glory's once again the fairy godmother, and I'm the Wicked Witch of the West. She's won, as usual."

I backed a step away. "You're wrong," I said. "You act like you and Glory are in some kind of contest over me, and you're not."

I should have stopped there, but I blurted out, "You blamed me for not being independent and not standing up for what I believe in, but you don't either. You do what Glory wants you to do. You care what Glory thinks."

Now I've done it, I thought. *I've ruined everything.* I took a deep breath and said to Mom, "I'm sorry about the party, Mom. You're right. I should have telephoned to ask you to take me home. If I'd known that one of their neighbors would call the police—"

"That's your only reason?"

"No—no," I stammered in surprise. "That's not what I meant."

"That's what you *said*."

I groaned. "Mom, I don't want to argue any-more. I said I was sorry. I won't make the same mis-take again. Can't we let it drop?"

Mom turned from the window and began to walk across the room toward the hallway. "Check your clothes," she said quietly. "See what needs laundering before you pack."

I sighed. "Mom, I already apologized. I'm sorry. What else can I say?"

Mom went on as though I hadn't said a word. "You need a new pair of dress shoes. We can run over to Dillard's this afternoon and buy them."

"Okay. Fine," I answered. Without another word I followed Mom to the doorway. If she wasn't going to give in, then I wouldn't either.

A flight attendant rolled her beverage cart to our row and smiled at me. "What would you like to drink?" she asked.

I asked for a Coke, and as I poured it over a cup of ice I made a decision. I'd telephone Mom when we reached the Miami airport. While everyone was waiting for their luggage, I could get away from Glory and talk to Mom in privacy. I began to feel better and the tight place under my ribs slid away. I'd definitely call Mom.

Later, in the airport, while the driver of the cruise ship's van was collecting our luggage, I found a nearby telephone and made the call, but all I got was Mom's recorded message. I stared at the phone, disappointed and upset.

"Rosie! Hurry up!" Glory shouted at me.

"It's me, Mom. I love you," I said to the machine, and hung up the phone. I ran to join the others, who were climbing into the van.

⌒――⌒

"Look at that ship! It's gigantic!" I exclaimed. As the van approached the Miami harbor, the ship loomed over the waterfront buildings.

Mrs. Eloise Fleming, the oldest member of Glory's bridge club, was squeezed in next to me. She leaned forward, squinting. "What's gigantic?" she shouted.

Neil Fleming, her seventeen-year-old grandson, who sat across the aisle, tapped her shoulder and said, "You're looking in the wrong direction, Grandma. The ship's over there."

Neil was close to six feet tall, but he sat slightly round-shouldered, as if he were used to hunching over a computer keyboard. His thick hair was dark. In my opinion it was cut and combed all wrong. His eyes, which were a deep blue, looked faded behind the glare of his wire-rimmed glasses. He was wearing a long-sleeved Hawaiian shirt, printed with pink flamingos and red hibiscus. I hoped his grandmother had picked it out.

"Neil knows all there is to know about our

ship," Mrs. Fleming bragged. She adjusted her hearing aid, then said, "Tell us, Neil."

He didn't seem bashful or embarrassed. As if on cue, he said, "It's fourteen decks above water level, four decks below." He raised his voice until his grandmother nodded that she could hear. "The ship's length is one thousand and twenty feet, its beam is a little over one hundred and fifty-seven feet, and its gross tonnage is one hundred and forty-two thousand tons."

"Isn't he wonderful?" Mrs. Fleming gurgled. "Four-point-plus grade average at school, of course."

"I know you're very proud of him," Glory said. She gave me a knowing look.

I didn't say a word. I focused on *not* saying what I was thinking. It was obvious that Glory had known Neil would accompany his grandmother on this trip. It was also obvious that Neil—one of the school's superbrained geeks in the class ahead of mine, who'd have no use for someone like me—was a guy Glory thought of as the "right kind" of date.

Forget it, I thought, shaken by the sudden realization that Glory's ideas were no better than Mom's.

At the thought of my mother I felt another pang. I resented the fact that Mom hadn't been forgiving or understanding by the time Glory and I had gotten on the plane. But of course I had to admit that I hadn't tried to ease the problem between us either.

Frustrated, I pushed the miserable feelings away. I was going on a cruise! It was a time for fun. I might never be able to convince Mom that I could courageously stand up for what I believed in, but I'd do my best to work things out with her later.

Neil broke into my thoughts. "The ship can carry a full load of more than three thousand passengers, and its total crew is one thousand one hundred and eighty."

Glory was looking at me, so I said the only thing that came into my head. "Wow."

"What did she say?" Mrs. Fleming asked.

"Wow!" I repeated, this time more loudly.

That seemed to satisfy everyone, including Neil's grandmother, who began to complain about her ophthalmologist. "At least I can still see the cards," she said, "and with Neil on hand to push my wheelchair when it's too far to walk, I should have no problems on this cruise."

As the van pulled into a parking space next to the boarding area, I leaned against the window, staring at a row of four gleaming cruise ships. I'd be a passenger on the largest ship of all. Since it was spring break, there were bound to be other kids on board. No matter what Glory had in mind about matching me with the "right kind" of boy, it was obvious that Neil wasn't interested, and neither was I. It was going to be hard enough just finding something we could talk about.

The van came to a stop next to a long, low terminal. With Glory's carry-on bag in one hand

and my own in the other, I climbed from the van and stared up at the ship we'd soon be boarding. "It's even bigger up close," I murmured.

"It has two large swimming pools and a theater that's five decks tall," Neil said.

"Wow," I repeated. This time I meant it.

I had to smile as I remembered my telephone conversation with my best friend, Becca, the night before. When she heard I was going on a cruise, she got excited. "Wow! It'll be like being on the *Titanic*!" she'd said. She loved that movie so much we'd seen it in the theater eight times and rented it seven.

"Not the *Titanic*," I'd answered. "There are no icebergs in the Caribbean."

"But just the same, you'll be on a great big, gorgeous ship. Does it have a sweeping staircase?"

"I don't know."

"I bet it does. You're going to look great gliding down the staircase in your formal gown while he watches you adoringly."

"While *who* watches me?"

"I don't know his name," Becca said, "but you're bound to meet him—your one true love. You're going on a glamorous ship with a sweeping staircase, and your name is Rose. It's fate."

"I'm too young to meet my one true love," I said.

"You're sixteen—almost seventeen. Rose Calvert

was only seventeen when she traveled on the *Titanic*."

I couldn't help laughing as she asked, "Are you going to stand in the prow with your arms stretched wide?"

"Oh, sure," I said. "All by myself."

"Not by yourself. With *him*. I want to know every detail when you get back. You'll tell me everything."

"I will," I answered. "I always tell you everything."

But I didn't tell her about my argument with Mom. It hurt too much to talk about.

———

As Neil took his grandmother's elbow and gently led her to her wheelchair, Glory called from the open doorway of the terminal, "Rosie! Have you got my carry-on?"

I turned so quickly that I collided with a squarely built, muscular man. He staggered a few steps, then caught his balance. "Oh! I'm so sorry," I said as I realized I'd bumped into a man who was probably somewhere in his late sixties.

"It is quite all right," the man said, smiling. He politely touched the brim of the straw hat he was wearing, then motioned to a teenage boy who was standing off to one side. "Ricky, *venga. Ahora, hijo.*"

Ricky, wearing a Cincinnati Reds baseball cap pulled low over his eyes, didn't respond at first, but as the man snapped "Ricky!" again, the startled boy hurried to his side, grabbed his carry-on bag, and strode with him into the terminal.

Neil pushed his grandmother's wheelchair to where I was standing. "His face is familiar," Neil said.

"Ricky's?" I asked as we entered the terminal, repeating the name I'd just heard. "Maybe you saw him at the airport."

"No," Neil said. "The older guy's. I know I've seen his face before."

I had no answer for him. Eager to enter the ship, I quickly followed Glory and her friends up the long ramp that led to the top of the terminal.

"What's the bottleneck?" Mrs. Fleming asked as we came to a stop behind a large group of passengers. "Why has everybody stopped here?"

"They're taking the passengers' pictures, Grandma," Neil answered.

With the ship as background through the open window, passengers were posing in groups, smiling or giggling as their pictures were taken by the ship's photographer. The man I had bumped into earlier, however, was vigorously shaking his head. He propelled Ricky around the group and up the gangway to the ship's entrance.

"He doesn't want their picture taken," Neil said, and I realized he'd been watching them too.

"I understand enough Spanish to know that he called Ricky 'son,' " I told Neil. "But Ricky seems to be only about our age. Do you think he's really the man's son?"

"Probably more like his grandson," Neil said. He quoted some statistics he'd recently read about the number of children and teenagers traveling with grandparents instead of parents, but I wasn't interested. The last thing in the world I wanted to be was part of a statistic.

I smiled for the camera, cheek to cheek with Glory, then started up the gangway. I would soon set foot on this gigantic, glamorous ship, and I was jumpy with excitement.

Glory fished in her large handbag and pulled out the preboarding papers she'd been given at the airport. As she handed my papers to me, I stepped to one side. At that second someone bumped into me so hard I stumbled backward.

"Lo siento," the boy named Ricky mumbled. He stopped in his dash down the gangway, reached out, and grabbed my shoulders, keeping me from falling.

"That's all right," I told him as I caught my balance. I wondered about the wary, almost fearful look in his eyes. "You were ahead of us. I thought you were already checked in. Aren't you going the wrong way?"

Ricky shrugged. *"Mi chaqueta*—my jacket. I forgot," he said, and began edging away.

The older man took a few steps toward us. "My sister-in-law's grandson left his jacket on a bench outside the terminal," he explained. He frowned at

Ricky, and I saw the same caution in his expression. "Go. Hurry," he said in English, and Ricky scurried down the gangway, careful not to collide with anyone else in the crowd of people moving toward the ship.

The man walked back onto the ship, holding up a blue plastic card the size of a credit card. A woman in a trim uniform glanced at the card, then motioned to him to enter.

As I reached the doorway, the woman asked the members of our group for their papers, then gave each of us similar blue plastic cards.

"These cards are your identification, your room key, and your charge card for anything you purchase on the ship," the woman said. "Always take them with you when you go ashore because they're your means of returning to the ship after a visit to one of the ports. In fact, keep them with you at all times."

As I tucked my card into my wallet, I noticed Neil craning his neck to look ahead. "I don't see him—Ricky's uncle," he said. "And I wanted to ask him something."

"What?" I asked.

"If he ever—oh, there he is."

Neil hurried to join the man, who was standing at the nearby elevator bank, and I heard him ask, "Did you ever play professional baseball?"

The man stiffened. For a moment his face was tight with what looked like fear. "What makes you ask a question like that?" he countered.

Neil shrugged. "I'm a baseball fan. I started by getting interested in the game when I was a little kid. Then I began memorizing statistics and collecting photos of the players and teams—you know, getting autographs and baseballs and all that stuff. I read a lot about baseball players. When I saw your nephew wearing that Cincinnati Reds cap—well, it helped me remember. Aren't you Martín Urbino, who used to play third base for the Reds?"

"No!" The man's answer was brusque to the point of rudeness, and I looked up, surprised.

As if trying to make up for his attitude, the man began to speak quietly and politely. "You have me confused with someone else, son. I am José Diago, and I have nothing to do with baseball. I operate an imports shop in Boston."

An elevator door opened and people swarmed inside, Mr. Diago with them. His head was down as though he was afraid of looking anyone in the eye.

Weird, I thought, but then an idea hit me that was even weirder.

"HE DIDN'T WAIT FOR HIS NEPHEW TO COME BACK," I
told Neil.

"He didn't have to," Neil said. "They both have
their card-keys, and we all know our stateroom
numbers from the packets that were mailed ahead
of time. Ricky can get to his stateroom without
any problem."

"Who was that man, Neil?" Mrs. Fleming
shouted. "And who's coming back?"

"Just somebody I was saying hello to, Grandma,"
Neil answered.

For a moment she looked confused, but Glory
stepped up, with the rest of the group right behind
her. "Have y'all got copies of the list of our stateroom numbers?" Glory asked.

"I think you typed in a mistake," Dora Duncastle said. "We're all supposed to be near each other on deck seven, but Eloise and Neil are listed as room thirteen hundred. Isn't the one in that number supposed to be a seven?"

Petite Betty Norwich elbowed Mrs. Duncastle and whispered, "Eloise booked one of those big two-bedroom suites that cost a fortune. It's up on the tenth deck."

Mrs. Duncastle raised an eyebrow, but no one said anything. Neil looked away, studying the designs on the wall as if he hadn't heard what had been said.

One of the elevators arrived nearly empty, and I thankfully joined the others, crowding inside.

Glory smiled at me and asked, "After lunch, while Eloise is resting, why don't you and Neil explore the ship and see what fun things there are to do?"

I didn't dare look in Neil's direction. I was going to have to have a long talk with my grandmother.

"We may as well have lunch right away," Mrs. Duncastle said. "That ship's attendant who met us at the airport said it takes a long time to get all the baggage delivered to the staterooms, so we can't unpack. Let's just drop our carry-ons in our rooms and meet in the café."

A few minutes later, as Glory and I stood outside the door of our stateroom, 7278, I said, "Glory, there are people everywhere to take care of your baggage and whatever you need. You didn't really need me to come along to help you. Did you invite me to come on the cruise just to meet Neil?"

"Of course not," Glory answered. "But it occurred to me when you were getting scolded about that party—and you should have been—that meeting a nice boy like Neil would be good for you."

"Neil is a brain."

"What's wrong with being intelligent?"

"Nothing. Except I'm not in Neil's league. He wouldn't be interested in me. And I'm not interested in him or in all that stuff he knows—especially not all those statistics he rattles off."

"Don't be silly," Glory said. She put her plastic card in the slot and opened the door. "Neil was only answering his grandmother's questions."

"She brags about him."

"Of course she does. All grandmothers brag. I brag about you. Let's go inside and take a look at our stateroom. We even have our own little balcony."

As I stepped back to move out of Glory's way, I heard a sharp intake of breath and realized I had stepped on someone's foot.

"I'm sorry," I said, regaining my balance. I quickly turned and saw Mr. Diago shutting the door of his interior stateroom, which was opposite ours.

"It is of no importance," Mr. Diago said. He checked to make sure the door was locked. "These passageways are narrow."

Realizing that Glory was watching from our

doorway, I introduced Mr. Diago. Then I asked him, "Did you find your nephew?"

"My nephew?" For a moment Mr. Diago seemed flustered. "Oh, yes. Ricky. He is here on the ship."

"Then I guess he got his jacket and made it back all right."

"Of course." He shrugged. "There was no need for concern." He tipped his straw hat to Glory, said, "I am pleased to have met you," and walked quickly down the passageway.

"Who is Mr. Diago? Where did you meet him?" Glory asked as soon as we entered the stateroom.

I didn't answer for a moment. I was captivated by the beauty of our stateroom. The blues and grays seemed to draw in the sea and sky. Opposite me was a wall of glass with a sliding door that opened onto a private balcony. The stateroom was small and compact, but I loved it.

"Well?" Glory asked.

I hurried to answer. "He's just someone traveling with his nephew." I put the bags on the two twin beds. "I bumped into him, his nephew nearly knocked me down, and I stepped on his foot." I giggled. "I hope we don't continue meeting like that."

Glory put an arm around my shoulders. "It's past one o'clock, and we're both starving," she said. "Let's join the others in the café and have lunch."

A few minutes later, after I'd gone through the serving line and was seated between Glory and Neil—how had Glory managed to do that?—I noticed Mr. Diago seated at a nearby table against the wall. Most tables had been quickly filled, with seats taken the moment they became empty, and his table was no exception. But there was no sign of Ricky, not even an empty seat saved for him.

I knew from having read the preboarding instructions on the plane that this large café was the only place on the ship to get lunch before we sailed. The main dining room, the small specialty restaurants, and the fast-food diners and ice cream bars were closed for this first, informal meal on the ship.

I gave a quick glance to the heaped plate Neil had prepared for himself. It was a well-known fact that teenage boys were always hungry, so Ricky was bound to be. Mr. Diago was bent over his plate, looking as if he were concentrating on his food and nothing else. Where was Ricky? Obviously his uncle didn't care.

I turned toward Neil, deciding to tell him about Mr. Diago's odd behavior, but Neil was listening to Mrs. Duncastle. I heard her say, "My father never missed a major baseball game. If it wasn't TV, then it was radio. I took in every game right along with him. So it was only natural, I suppose, that my late husband was also a baseball fan."

"Did you follow the Cincinnati Reds?" Neil asked.

"Yes, but they weren't my favorites." She giggled and added, "Don't ask me why, as a native west Texan, I rooted for the Minnesota Twins. I still remember 1965—before you were born—and the Cuban stars who brought the Twins the pennant—Tony Oliva, Sandy Valdespino, and Camilo Pascual. Pascual was one of the best pitchers in the majors."

"Don't forget Zoilo Versalles, a top shortstop with a great batting average."

Mrs. Duncastle swallowed a large bite of potato salad and said, "Those Cubans really made a name for themselves. I still remember Cookie Rojas. He was with the Phillies and ended up managing the Angels in 1988."

"There was another Cuban star—Martín Urbino," Neil said. "Remember him? He was a good all-around player and went on to manage one of the Cincinnati Reds' minor-league teams."

"I remember Urbino," Mrs. Duncastle said. "Stocky and strong. He had a lot of power behind that bat."

"Take a look at the man facing us at the table next to the wall," Neil said. "Doesn't he look like Martín Urbino?"

Mrs. Duncastle put on her glasses and leaned forward. "Where?" she asked.

Neil turned to point him out. I looked too, but Mr. Diago was no longer there. A young blond woman sat in the chair where he had been. She was eating and chatting with the woman next to her.

"I guess he left," Neil said. "Well, it doesn't matter. If I see him later, I'll point him out to you."

As Neil and Mrs. Duncastle went back to

discussing baseball, I turned to Glory on my other side. But she was busy listening to a detailed complaint from Myra Evans about her son-in-law.

I finished my salad, my thoughts on Mom. They were bound to have postcards on the ship. I'd send one to Mom, just to let her know I was thinking about her. To say I was sorry we'd parted on such unhappy terms. To say . . . I put my napkin on the table and began to slide my chair back.

I was about to excuse myself when a tall, muscular man who was probably in his mid-sixties stopped behind my chair, blocking my way.

"Dora?" he asked Mrs. Duncastle in a voice so deep it sounded like the voice of a bear in a Saturday-morning cartoon. "Is it really you?"

Mrs. Duncastle turned, looking up with surprise. She beamed, a tiny speck of broccoli decorating her smile. "Anthony Bailey!" she said, grasping his hand. "I haven't seen you since Fred and I had dinner with you at that builders' convention in Las Vegas."

"How is your husband?"

"Oh, Fred's fine. Enjoying retirement." Without letting go of Mr. Bailey's hand, Mrs. Duncastle introduced him to everyone at the table and giggled. "I was so impressed because Anthony was staying in the Las Vegas hotel's presidential suite."

He tried to look modest but didn't make it as he said, "This time it's the *royal* suite—top of the line."

"Oh, my," Mrs. Duncastle said, sounding impressed all over again. Then she asked Mr. Bailey,
"Are you on board for the bridge tournament?"

He laughed. "No. Bridge is not my game. To my
way of thinking, playing cards for fun, as you once
put it, is a waste of time."

"I hope you're kidding," Glory began, but Mr.
Bailey interrupted her by holding up his free hand.

"Ladies, I own a company that builds and oper-
ates casinos. You can see why I said what I did." He
laughed in a low rumble, and some of the women
smiled in return.

"Do you manage the casino on this ship?" Mrs.
Duncastle asked.

He shook his head. "No, but my associates and I
have been discussing the possibility of establishing
cruises exclusively for gambling. Excursions in various ports would also be connected to casinos. This
is not strictly a pleasure trip for me, since I'm on
this cruise as an observer."

Neil swiveled in his chair so that he could look
up at Mr. Bailey. "How many Caribbean ports besides Havana have gambling casinos?"

"Not enough," Mr. Bailey answered. "But it's a
problem my company can easily remedy, given the
right cooperation. As for Cuba, I've already made
initial contact with authorities in Castro's government. Eventually, when the tourist trade with
the United States is fully restored, I hope to get

permission to build and develop a Havana casino that will put any Vegas casino in a backseat."

"Do you enjoy gambling, Mr. Bailey?" Alicia Carver asked.

Neil spoke before Mr. Bailey could answer. "In any casino the odds are always in favor of the house," he said. "I could give you statistics, but Mr. Bailey probably knows them. I'm sure he doesn't gamble."

Mr. Bailey chuckled. "Only on a sure thing, kid," he said. "I make it a point never to pass up a sure thing."

He pulled his hand from Mrs. Duncastle's grip and patted her shoulder. "I look forward to seeing you and your friends again on this trip," he said.

Mrs. Duncastle gave him time to leave the café, then said, almost purring, "Anthony is such a nice, friendly person."

"Handsome, too," Mrs. Applebee said. "Did you notice that the polo shirt he was wearing matched the blue of his eyes?"

"I think he was flirting with you, Dora." Mrs. Carver giggled.

"Nonsense," Mrs. Duncastle said, but she giggled too.

"What's so funny?" Mrs. Fleming asked as she adjusted her hearing aid. "And who was that man?"

"Dora's good-looking boyfriend," Glory answered, and all the women laughed.

I couldn't take any more of their silliness. It was embarrassing to hear grandmothers talking about boyfriends. "Please excuse me," I said, pushing back my chair. "I have to buy a postcard."

Glory leaned forward. "Neil, why don't you go with Rosie? I'll take Eloise to her stateroom and see that she's comfortable. That will give you two a chance to look over the ship."

The back of Neil's neck turned red as he said, "No thank you, Mrs. Marstead. Maybe some other time, but I promised Grandma I'd look out for her, and I'd feel better about it if I stayed with her at first."

Was every guy I met going to reject me? Uncomfortable because all the women were watching, I quickly said, "It's okay, Glory. I'll see you soon. Excuse me, please." I strode away from the table to the nearest elevator bank. I'd go to the desk on deck five, where I could probably get a postcard with a picture of the ship.

A girl with long brown hair was the only occupant of the elevator. She wore a sheer pale blue blouse over a white tank top and shorts. *I wish I looked that cool,* I thought. "Hi," the girl said as I got in.

"Hi," I answered automatically.

"Are you going to Star Struck?" She pulled her I.D. card out of her blouse pocket, examined it, then put it back.

I shook my head. "No, I'm going to deck five."

It suddenly dawned on me what she had said, and I asked, "What's Star Struck?"

"It's the hangout they've got on board for teenagers. It's on deck twelve."

"Don't tell me," I said, and made a face. "Crafts and other so-called fun stuff designed to keep us busy."

"No. It's not like that. It's a cool place. And almost every night there's a band with some pretty good music."

The elevator doors began to close. The girl took a step forward, then paused, brushing back her hair. She let the door close again. "Never mind. I'll ride down to five with you," she said. "My name is Julieta Vargas."

"I'm Rosie Marstead," I answered.

"Sixteen? Seventeen?"

"Sixteen."

"Me too." Julieta leaned back against the elevator wall and sighed with relief. "I'm glad you're aboard. I've been wandering around looking, but I've only met thirteen- and fourteen-year-olds so far."

The elevator stopped at deck five, and I said, "Here's where I get out."

"Are you going shopping? Mind if I go with you?"

"Sure." I smiled, feeling much better. Here was someone my own age who wanted to be friends. I didn't need Neil, and—no matter what Becca had predicted—I wasn't looking for romance.

At the desk I asked for a postcard of the ship, bought a stamp for it, then tried to think of a quick message that would fit. I needed to write something that would tell Mom exactly how I felt and how much I really loved her.

Julieta watched, impatiently shifting from one foot to the other, but I tried not to let it bother me. I thought hard, but what could I really say on a postcard, open for anyone to read? I finally wrote, *Dear Mom, This is a beautiful ship. I wish you were here. I love you. Rose Ann.*

It wasn't what I'd hoped to write, but it would do. I'd write another postcard later, when I had time to really think about what to say. I dropped it into the ship's mailbox and walked with Julieta into the mall.

"When the ship sails at five, there'll be a calypso band on deck eleven, by the outside swimming pool," Julieta said. "They're having a *bon voyage* party."

"How do you know all this?" I asked. We stepped into a shop that had racks of jackets, sweatshirts, and T-shirts—all with the ship's name and logo on them.

"How do I know all this?" Julieta shrugged. "My parents and I live in Miami, so we go cruising every year. By now I've learned the drill." She bent over a jewelry counter. "Pretty," she said, pointing to some twisted gold costume-jewelry rings.

But what caught my eye were pendants—silver replicas of sunken treasure edged in gold. "How much?" I asked the woman behind the counter. I knew Mom would love one of those.

"The small ones are thirty-five dollars," the woman answered. "They go up in price according to size. Each comes with a certificate."

"Thanks," I said, and turned away. Thirty-five dollars? That would be nearly all my spending money.

I spotted Mr. Diago at the far end of the shop buying a navy blue T-shirt. Ricky still wasn't with him. "Julieta," I said, "if you know a lot about cruising, then you'll know the answer to this. Could anyone get lost on board this ship?"

"Lost like you don't show up for dinner on time, because you're still in the pool?"

"No. I mean lost period. Like no one would know if you were on the ship or not."

"A stowaway? I don't think so. No one gets on board without an identification card, and there are security people all over the place."

"I didn't mean like a stowaway," I said.

Julieta tilted her head and studied me with a puzzled look on her face. "Well, what *did* you mean?"

"I don't know," I said. "I've never been on a cruise ship before, and I suppose I was just thinking about how big this ship is." I didn't want to tell

Julieta about Mr. Diago. I didn't know her well enough. I wasn't even sure what I was suspicious of yet. I wished Becca were on board to talk to.

Julieta and I visited all the shops on the promenade, stopping to refuel at the serve-yourself ice cream bar.

We were just finishing our cones when we heard an announcement that everyone aboard ship was required to be at their proper station for the compulsory lifeboat muster.

"As soon as it's over, meet me on deck eleven so we can hear the calypso band while we sail out of the harbor," Julieta said.

"Okay," I answered. My heart beat faster with excitement. We were almost ready to sail! I hurried to our stateroom and saw that only one of the bright orange life jackets was still on the bed. Glory was probably already wearing hers.

I read the instructions, pulled on the bulky life jacket, and hurried to our assigned station on deck four, where the crowd of passengers searching for their places on deck moved like a swarm of fat orange bees.

For a moment I remembered the terrible scene in *Titanic* when people scrambled for lifeboats and there weren't enough places, and Rose Calvert and Jack Dawson . . . I groaned. The last thing I wanted—or would ever get—was a gorgeous Jack Dawson. And anyway, Rose and Jack didn't live happily ever after.

I paused in the doorway to the outer deck, looking for Glory, and overheard someone grumble, "I haven't got time for this rubbish. I should be on deck eleven setting up. Nobody told me there was going to be so much to do."

I glanced to one side, where a lean, blond man wearing gray slacks and a light blue polo shirt was struggling to strap on his life vest.

The pretty young woman next to him, wearing the ship's uniform, raised one eyebrow. "Don't tell me this is your first job as a cruise director, Tommy."

Tommy stopped and scowled. "I'm a last-minute sub, okay? Your company's VP had to take whoever he could get. Your regular cruise director should have picked a more convenient time to fall off the stage and break his arm."

The woman laughed. "Poor Jerry. And poor Tommy. All week you'll be on energy overload, and you won't get much sleep."

"Thanks for the encouragement," he grumbled. "If Broadway hadn't been totally dead for comedians this season, I would have turned this gig down."

"Where on Broadway would you get the chance to lead a group of six-A.M. joggers around the top deck each morning?" She looked as if she was enjoying the conversation, and I wondered if this last-minute cruise director wasn't too popular with the rest of the crew. What could be worse than a comedian with no sense of humor?

Tommy stopped scowling. He leaned against one of the lifeboat supports and flashed a smile at the woman. "After the show closes tonight, I'm hosting a little party in my cabin," he said. "It's room eleven-oh-five. Wanna come?"

"Ask Rita," she said.

"Who's Rita?"

The woman's grin was pure mischief. "That short, cute room steward on deck seven. She likes your looks, and she thinks you're a Broadway star."

"Rosie, there you are!" Glory came up behind me and clutched my arm. "We're all down at station seven. Come with me, sweetie. Hurry!"

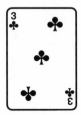

WE JOINED THE OTHERS AT OUR STATION IN TIME TO line up as ordered and listen to instructions about evacuating the ship. It didn't take long, and as soon as everyone had been dismissed, I asked, "Glory, may I go to deck eleven and listen to a calypso band?"

"Of course," Glory said. She stood on tiptoe to scan the group, which was quickly disbanding.

"Neil already left with his grandmother," I told her.

Glory didn't even bother looking embarrassed. "I thought he'd enjoy going with you," she said.

I didn't argue. I walked with Glory to our stateroom, stowed the life jacket in the closet, fished my

Polaroid camera from my carry-on, then hurried up to deck eleven, where Julieta was waiting.

The cruise director I'd seen at the drill bounded through the waiting crowd onto a makeshift stage and introduced himself as Tommy Jansen, star of Broadway and TV. The stiff breeze blew his hair into his eyes as he tried to tell a joke about losing more than one toupee overboard. I didn't laugh at the joke, and neither did most of the others crowded around the stage.

Finally Jansen introduced the band members, who swung into their first selection before he jumped from the stage.

I smiled as Julieta immediately began bouncing to the calypso beat. "This reminds me of the Cuban music in that movie *Buena Vista Social Club*," I said.

Julieta suddenly stiffened. In a firm voice she insisted, "It's *not* Cuban music. It's calypso."

Surprised, I tried to explain. "I thought . . . that is, well, I mean since we're going to sail near Cuba . . ."

Julieta turned and leaned on the rail. "Don't talk about Cuba to me. My parents escaped from Cuba to the United States when Fidel Castro came into power. They had to leave everything behind and start over."

I took a step backward, not knowing how to answer. "Your parents must have done well in the United States. You told me you go cruising every year."

"My father is an orthodontist. He has a good practice," Julieta said, but as she stepped away from the rail, she bristled with anger. "You couldn't know what it has been like to be an exile. I was never able to meet any of my grandparents. I never had the chance to sit on their laps or feel their hugs. There were phone calls and letters, but that was not enough. My parents sent American money so my grandparents could shop at the Cuban dollar stores and buy things to make life comfortable, but my grandparents couldn't leave Cuba, and we couldn't go back. During the past few years all four of my grandparents died. Now I'll never . . . don't say another word about Cuba. I don't even want to *think* about Cuba."

Julieta leaned again on the railing, and I joined her. I hadn't meant to make her angry, and I was still surprised at how upset she had become. "I'm sorry," I said. "I didn't know any of this, but now that I do—"

"It's okay. Forget about it," Julieta interrupted. She took a deep breath and acted as if we hadn't had the conversation about Cuba at all. "Look at the Miami skyline as we sail out of the harbor," she said pleasantly. "I've seen it so many times, but it always looks so white and clean and beautiful."

"Sun-soaked," I said as I took a couple of pictures.

Julieta smiled. "Yes," she said. "That's a good way to put it. Miami is sun-soaked."

We watched the shoreline until it disappeared. I barely made it back to the stateroom in time to change before dinner.

———

Dinner was elegant, and the table we'd been assigned was just below the golden, sweeping double staircase. I leaned back in my chair, closing my eyes for a moment, absorbed by the soft background music of harp and piano. The romantic music, the glittering light from the many chandeliers, the train of a long gown trailing behind me as I gracefully descended the stairs . . .

Mrs. Carver leaned across the table, asking loudly, "Are you okay, Rosie? You have a funny look on your face. It's probably that spicy shrimp cocktail sauce acting up. It gets me every time."

I felt a rush of warmth to my face. Becca and her *Titanic* dreams of romance. They were hers, not mine, and I had to keep them from capturing me. "I'm fine," I said. "I was just, um—enjoying the music."

As the waiter brought our desserts, Glory leaned forward, turning to address everyone at the table. "Listen, y'all, as soon as we finish, let's go to the Welcome Aboard show in the theater. It begins in half an hour."

"Show" seemed to be the magic word. All the

women at the table began talking eagerly about shipboard shows and dinner-theater shows and Broadway shows. I enjoyed my absolutely guaranteed low-fat chocolate éclair and kept myself from asking for another one. I really didn't want to see whatever Tommy Jansen had dreamed up for a welcome show, but this was Glory's trip. I reminded myself that I was here to "help" Glory. And I'd been spared having to spend time with Neil. He was half turned away, talking with his grandmother. Good.

But later, after the welcome show—a busy hour with dancers, singers, and a short speech from the captain—all the bridge players declared their intention of going to bed early.

"We want to be in top condition when the tournament begins tomorrow morning," Mrs. Applebee said.

I rebelled. Past the huge windows the sea stretched into a dark, mysterious void, but the ship was alive with lights and laughter and music. I didn't want to leave it. Impulsively, I turned to Neil, who was standing near me. "There's still so much to see and do. Come with me. Let's check out the disco."

For an instant Neil looked panic-stricken. He swallowed hard, cleared his throat, and said, "No thanks, Rosie. I'd better stick with Grandma."

I shrugged, trying to hide the frustration I felt at asking and getting turned down. "Okay," I said. I began to leave, but Neil surprised me by putting a hand on my shoulder.

"Uh, Rosie . . . , wait," he said. "Uh, how about . . . uh, could we do something tomorrow?"

"Tomorrow?" I wanted to tell Neil that I didn't care what he did, but I saw Glory watching, and the courage to say what was on my mind vanished. "Okay," I answered. "Tomorrow will be fine."

⌒——⌒

The next day—Monday—was a day at sea. The ship wouldn't reach its first port, Bonita Beach, until early Tuesday morning. The bridge tournament began at ten A.M., so with Glory's blessing I was free to swim, get some sun, and join in a volleyball game.

Julieta and I met at the pool and sat in the shade to enjoy a lunch of hamburgers and fries. To my surprise, Neil joined us.

"Hi," he said. "Your grandmother said you might be up here." He perched uncomfortably on the end of the long chaise I was sitting on, facing me, but as he looked at me his cheeks turned red. He quickly looked away.

I caught the spark of interest in Julieta's eyes as she was introduced to Neil. I had to admit that in swim trunks and without a gaudy Hawaiian shirt, Neil looked pretty cool.

"Want to swim?" Julieta asked him.

"That's why I'm here," he said, and Julieta

laughed as though he'd come up with something clever.

As Julieta stood up, pulling off the shirt she'd thrown on over a brief red bikini, I asked, "Don't you want to finish your lunch, Julieta?"

"I've had enough," she said. She took Neil's hand and pulled him over to the swimming pool.

I munched on my hamburger. If Julieta wanted Neil, she could have him. I didn't care.

Glory suddenly appeared, a scarf over her head and extralarge sunglasses resting on her nose. She slid onto the chaise Julieta had vacated. "Hi," she said.

"Hi," I answered. "Want something to eat?"

"No thanks," Glory said. She pushed Julieta's plate aside. "We had a lunch buffet and we're on a short break. How are things going?"

"This ship is fabulous," I said, and grinned at her. "Thanks again, Glory."

"You don't need to thank me. You're doing *me* a favor. Remember?"

I laughed. "I'd be able to help if you'd tell me what I can do for you."

"You can pay attention to that nice boy, Neil. Where is he, by the way?"

"In the pool."

"Is this his hamburger?"

"No," I answered. "It's Julieta's. She's a girl I met yesterday. She's swimming with Neil."

Glory turned to gaze at the pool, and I did too.

Julieta and Neil were playing some kind of water tag, laughing and splashing and obviously having fun.

Glory faced me, peering over the top of her sunglasses. "You need to get into the game, Rosie," she said.

"There's no point," I said. "Neil isn't interested in me, and I'm not interested in him."

"He could be," Glory answered. "And there's no reason for you not to be."

"But I'm not," I said. "Not in Neil, not in any guy. I've been dumped. I've been rejected. I've had enough."

The humiliation I'd experienced at that awful party returned so suddenly that I felt ill. I put down what was left of my hamburger.

"You're only sixteen and you're giving up? Nonsense," Glory said. "There are many nice guys in this world—guys like Neil. Tomorrow I'm going to see that the two of you take the first tender to Bonita Beach. With Eloise's blessing, I've signed you and Neil up for a snorkeling excursion."

"I don't know how to snorkel."

"Neither does Neil, according to Eloise. But I understand it's easy to learn."

I sighed. I was beginning to realize how hard it was for Mom to resist Glory when she had a goal in mind. "Are you going too?"

Glory stood and smoothed her cotton skirt. "Of

course not," she said. "I'm going to be doing my best to the win the bridge tournament. I drew Dora as my partner tomorrow, and we make a good team." She winked. "So will you and Neil. He's a much better person than that Cam Daly. Now, get in the pool and make Neil pay attention to you."

As she left, I sank back on the chaise and squeezed my eyes shut. I had no intention of competing with Julieta for a guy I wasn't even interested in and who didn't seem to be interested in me.

And as for tomorrow . . . it wasn't fair! A date that had been arranged by a pair of grandmothers? I was positive that Neil would hate it every bit as much as I would.

The next morning at eight-thirty I left the bright elevator for the narrow, dull, beige corridors of deck one and waited to board the first tender to Bonita Beach with Neil, who reeked of suntan lotion.

"Have fun!" Glory called to us from the sidelines.

"Neil, turn up your collar. Be careful not to get too much sun!" Mrs. Fleming shouted. "You know how easily you burn."

I pretended I didn't hear and saw that Neil was doing the same. Why didn't our grandmothers leave us alone?

A uniformed woman with a microphone announced, "Those who are signed up for the snorkel expedition, gather at pier B. Everyone who is planning to enjoy the beach activities, stop off at the booth with the thatched roof to pick up your bottled water."

I wished Neil would say something—anything—so our being together wouldn't seem so awkward, but he didn't, and I couldn't think of any small talk. To kill time, I glanced around at the others waiting in the narrow passage. To my surprise, I saw Mr. Diago, who was obviously alone, with no nephew in sight. As many of the passengers did, he carried a small sports bag. His was green with a sports logo on one side, and he was dressed in neatly pressed slacks and a white polo shirt. That was not the kind of outfit to wear for a day at the beach.

"Neil," I began, "there's something strange about—"

The woman speaking into the microphone overrode what I had hoped to say. "Form two straight lines as you board the tender," she called out. "Be sure you have your blue card. You won't be able to reboard the ship without it."

"What did you say?" Neil bent to ask me, but the crowd surged forward.

I shook my head. "I'll tell you later," I said, and glanced again at Mr. Diago, who was up ahead. I was growing more and more sure that Mr. Diago's nephew, Ricky, had not returned to the ship before it sailed. But Mr. Diago was pretending that he had. Why?

I followed Mr. Diago onto the boat, deliberately sitting beside him. "Good morning," I said.

"Good morning," he answered. His smile flickered, and his words were clipped. "We have good weather. It's a beautiful day."

"Yes indeed," I said. "By the way, Mr. Diago, where is Ricky?"

"Ricky slept late. He will be along soon," he answered. He looked away, toward the beach.

But by the time the boat pulled away from the pier, Ricky still hadn't joined us.

MUCH LATER, AFTER OUR MORNING OF SNORKELING, I climbed up the gangplank into the tour boat, turned in my snorkel gear, and accepted an oversized towel and a box lunch an attendant handed me. I spread my towel on a bench on the lower deck, which was open to the air but shaded by the deck above. The drops of water on my skin dried quickly, the salt drying and tickling, and an occasional rivulet from my wet hair felt good as it rolled down my back.

Neil suddenly stood in front of me. "Is it okay if I sit with you?"

I looked up, shading my eyes with my hand. He'd put on a long-sleeved shirt and a wide-brimmed straw hat.

"Sure," I said. "If you want to."

"Would you rather I didn't?"

"No, but don't think that you *have* to."

Neil plopped down next to me on his towel and opened his lunch. "This conversation could go on forever, and I'm hungry."

I tore open a small bag of potato chips as the boat's engines started up. "Look, I know my grandmother pushed us together, and I'm embarrassed about it. I wouldn't blame you if you didn't want to come anywhere near me."

Neil looked surprised. He chewed and gulped until he'd finished his mouthful of sandwich. "You've got the wrong idea. I was glad when we met on the plane and I knew you'd be on the tour. I'm just not very good at making small talk. I didn't know what to say to you."

"You talked to Julieta," I blurted out before I could stop myself. "Ohhh, forget I said that," I mumbled.

Neil shrugged. "Julieta talked to me. And she talked and she talked."

"About what?"

"I don't know. I tuned her out. You know, it's like when a radio station is playing in the background and you hear the music but you don't pay any attention to the words."

I laughed. Maybe I'd been wrong about Neil. "I like your hat and the way the brim curls down to cover your face and neck," I said. "I wish I had one like it."

"It came from a Caribbean cruise Grandma and Grandpa took years ago," Neil said. "There are probably some hats just like it for sale in the market at Bonita Beach." He grinned as he added, "Each of my Hawaiian shirts is one of a kind, though. No matter how much you wish you had one, you won't be able to get it. They probably haven't been made since the fifties."

Surprised, I said, "You don't like them? Then why do you wear them?"

"It makes Grandma happy. I really don't mind."

"You don't care what other people think?"

"No. Why should I?"

That's courage, I thought. I smiled at Neil and pointed toward the spit of land where the tender was docked. "Look. We're almost at the beach, and the tender's there. We can catch it without waiting half an hour."

But as the boat docked and we walked onto the pier, I saw someone waving at us.

Julieta, in a white bikini that set off her perfect tan, ran to meet us. "I've been looking all over for you," she said. "You didn't tell me you'd signed up for the snorkel tour."

"It was last-minute," I said.

Julieta grabbed Neil's right hand. "Well, come on, then. We'll make up for lost time. The water's perfect."

"I'm sorry. No more swimming for me," Neil said. He strode down the dock to where the tender was moored. "I've had enough sun for today. We're going back to the ship."

For an instant Julieta's lower lip curled out in a pout. "The ship won't sail for over three hours. Are you really going to let this beautiful beach go to waste?"

Neil shrugged and turned to look at me. "Rosie, do you want to stay and swim with Julieta?"

I shook my head. "I'm sorry, Julieta," I said. "We've been swimming all morning. I'm ready to go back too."

Julieta didn't let go of Neil's hand. "Getting out of the sun is probably a good idea. Besides, there's lots to do on the ship."

As we boarded the tender with a few other passengers, Neil paused. "I'll join you in a minute," he said. "I want to ask the pilot something about water depth and pressure."

Julieta waited with Neil, but I went ahead. I slid onto one of the long benches, resting my elbow on the rail, and gazed out over the water, now a deep blue glazed with gold.

Mom would have liked this trip, I thought. *I wish Glory had invited Mom, too.*

I sighed. No matter how angry I'd been at Mom, I couldn't help missing her. Maybe if I hadn't become so angry that I said what I shouldn't have, I could have finally explained to Mom that—

Someone slid in next to me, sitting so close that the wide brim of his hat grazed my head and I could feel the trembling in his thighs. He rested his right arm along the back of the bench behind me, as if we were together.

Startled, I turned, saying, "Neil, I—"

It wasn't Neil sitting beside me.

I looked into the face of a boy who seemed not much older than I. With his light golden skin, deep brown eyes, and dark hair, he was one of the best-looking guys I'd ever seen. Topping his swimming shorts was a navy blue T-shirt with the ship's crest in gleaming white, and he wore a broad-brimmed straw hat exactly like Neil's. He didn't smile.

"We have not met," he said, a Hispanic accent softening his words, "but please, may I sit with you?"

I nodded. He'd already made that decision.

"We have not been introduced. I do not know your name."

As if I'd been hypnotized, I answered, "I'm Rose Ann Marstead."

I expected him to tell me his name, but instead, he smiled and murmured, "Rose. A beautiful name."

I wished he'd say my name again. It was like a soft sigh, like a breeze rustling leaves. But instead, his next words jolted me like an electric shock.

"Rose, my name is Ricky Diago," he said.

I gave a start. This was definitely not the Ricky Diago I had met before the ship sailed. How likely would it be that there were *two* Ricky Diagos on the same ship? Cautiously, I said, "We met a Mr. José Diago on the ship. Is he your uncle?"

Ricky hesitated only a moment. "*Sí* . . . yes," he answered.

Now I was really confused. Ricky's gaze was steady, as if he were telling the truth, but I knew better. I'd had a close look at the Ricky Diago who had boarded with his uncle. He had grabbed me to keep me from falling when we'd collided on the gangway, and I had looked into his eyes. I had no trouble remembering him. This boy who called himself Ricky Diago was not the same person.

As Neil plopped down on the bench with Julieta behind him, Ricky twisted in his seat, and I felt something jostle my ankle. I looked down to see a green sports bag. It was the same color as the one Mr. Diago had been carrying. It even bore the same logo. Was it the same bag?

I wondered if Neil would remember the other Ricky. "Julieta . . . Neil," I said, "this is Ricky Diago. We've met his uncle—José Diago."

Julieta dimpled and said something to Ricky about hanging out together on the ship. Neil smiled and looked at Ricky with interest.

He doesn't realize it's not the same Ricky, I thought. I glanced at Julieta, who hadn't taken her eyes off Ricky. Now was not the time to try to tell Neil what I knew.

"Your uncle looks a lot like Martín Urbino, who used to play with the Cincinnati Reds," Neil said.

"Martín Urbino? I never heard of him," Ricky said quietly, but I could feel the muscles in his thigh jump, then tighten, and I saw that he was squeezing his fists so tightly that his knuckles were white.

The tender's motors started up with a low roar, and the boat moved away from the pier. Under cover of the noise, I leaned close to Ricky. Using all the courage I had, I whispered, "I met Ricky Diago when we boarded. I remember his face. You are *not* Ricky Diago. Who are you *really*?"

Ricky didn't answer. He stared straight ahead, as if he hadn't heard, but a vein in his temple throbbed.

As the tender reached the ship, Ricky turned to me. *"Por favor,"* he whispered. Desperately he gripped my arm and began again. "Please give me a chance. It means my life. Accept me as Ricky Diago. When it is possible I will explain to you."

The tender nudged the mooring station, and the few people who were aboard got to their feet, making their way to the stairway at the front of the boat.

I took a deep breath. The Ricky Diago I had first met had disappeared. I was sure now that he had never returned to the ship after giving the excuse of looking for his jacket. And here was a substitute, claiming both the name and the uncle. Maybe I was the only one who would recognize that this

Ricky was not the one who had checked in. What should I do?

Ricky's brown eyes pleaded with me as he whispered, "Please, Rose? Will you help me?"

"Rosie? Aren't you coming?" Neil called.

I nodded to Ricky. "I won't tell anyone . . . yet," I said. "But you're going to have to tell me the truth." I pulled my I.D. card from my shirt pocket, ready to show it to the uniformed attendant at the entrance to deck one. Surprised, I saw that Ricky was holding an I.D. card too.

With so little time left to spend on the beach, not many people were waiting to take the tender to shore. Among those were a few who were not dressed for the beach and who seemed to be simply looking over the passengers as they returned to the ship.

At the back was Anthony Bailey, the casino owner I remembered meeting the day before. His dark glasses concealed his eyes, and he showed no recognition of me as I walked toward him. That didn't surprise me. He'd been standing behind my chair as he talked to Mrs. Duncastle.

Beside him a ship's officer stood close to a man dressed in a khaki military uniform, complete with thick brass buttons on the jacket and a squared-off cap with a bill—the same kind of uniform I'd seen on Fidel Castro in pictures. The man's large gold ring, with a raised initial C, flashed in the bright light as he handed the officer a sheet of paper. The officer scanned it before studying the passengers.

Behind them stood Mr. Diago, almost hidden by the others. He seemed to be more intent on the conversation between the ship's officer and the man in the uniform than on the arriving passengers.

I nudged Ricky and said, "There's your uncle."

But Ricky ducked his head, his wide hat brim covering his face. "Say nothing," he whispered. He suddenly took my hand and stepped from the gangplank onto the deck of the ship.

As we held out our I.D. cards so the attendant could see them, Mr. Diago burst into a loud coughing fit. Off balance, he lurched against the man in the uniform, and for a few moments, as Ricky and I passed them, the man and the officer seemed concerned only with keeping Mr. Diago from falling.

As Ricky tugged me around a bend and onto an open elevator, I asked, "What's the matter with you, Ricky? Your uncle needed help. Why didn't you stop and help him?"

"He didn't need help," Ricky told her. "*I* did. I do."

"What are you talking about?"

"Please keep your voice down," Ricky begged. "I will tell you when I can. I promise to explain."

"Hey! Hold the door open!" Julieta shouted. She and Neil squeezed through the closing doors and into the elevator.

"Oh, sorry," I said. I caught Neil's puzzled

glance at my right hand, which Ricky was still gripping, and pulled it away. "We were talking and thought you were right behind us."

Neil looked pointedly at Ricky. "We stopped to make sure your uncle was all right."

"I knew he was," Ricky said. "He—he often has coughing fits. That is, they look worse than they are."

His excuse sounded lame to me, and probably to the others, because neither Neil nor Julieta answered. I was glad when we reached deck six and the doors opened. "My deck," Julieta said. "Anybody else getting out?"

When no one answered, she looked hopeful and asked, "Let's meet on eleven in an hour. Okay?"

"Okay," Neil said, but he looked at me.

I shrugged. "Fine with me," I answered.

As we reached deck seven, Ricky stepped out of the elevator. I said quietly to Neil, "I'll see you in just a little while. I've got something weird to tell you."

Neil gave a quick glance in Ricky's direction. "Call me," he said. "You know our suite number."

The passageway was nearly empty as Ricky and I walked the short distance to our staterooms. I opened the door to 7278 and turned to Ricky. "Well?" I asked him. "Do you want to tell me the truth now?"

Down the passageway the elevator doors opened. I heard the sound but ignored it.

Ricky didn't. His eyes widened, and for an instant he stiffened.

Then, to my amazement, instead of using his key to enter his uncle's stateroom, he pushed me into my stateroom and quickly shut the door. Before I realized what was happening, he grabbed me from behind and clapped a hand over my mouth.

"I think I am being followed," he whispered into my ear. "Do not call for help. Do not make a sound, I beg of you."

Held tightly against Ricky, I could feel the rapid pounding of his heart. Or was it my own heart that was so out of control? I had never been so frightened.

"You must not call out," Ricky whispered. "Will you help me?"

Agreeing with him seemed to be the only way to go, so I managed to nod assent, trembling as he released me and stepped aside.

"Will you check the passageway?" he asked. "Tell me if someone is there."

Obediently, I peered through the peephole. The short section of the passageway I could see was empty, but I slowly opened the door, clinging to it for support, and glanced to both sides.

I could run. I could scream for help, I told myself, wild thoughts zinging through my mind. But Ricky had made no move to harm me, and I could see that he was as frightened as I was. I silently shut the door and turned to Ricky, leaning against it. "The passageway is empty," I said.

Ricky closed his eyes, letting out a long, shuddering sigh.

"You said that someone is following you. Why?" I asked.

Dropping as though his legs no longer had the strength to hold him up, Ricky sat on the edge of one of the twin beds. "We hoped it would not happen," he said. "The boatman swore he would not tell."

"Tell what?" I asked.

Ricky looked at me, his eyes wide with fear. "Rose," he said, "I have escaped from Cuba to seek political asylum in the United States. Now I am being hunted by the government. If they find me, they'll take me back to Cuba, where I will be charged with desertion . . . a crime punishable by death."

I was shocked. "Desertion? That doesn't sound right. How old are you?"

"Seventeen. I'll be eighteen in May."

"Then surely the judge in your trial would—"

Ricky interrupted with a bitter laugh. "Trial? My case would come to trial only if the object would be to teach a lesson to others who try to escape the island. And it would not be the kind of trial that would take place in your country. It is more likely that I would be taken quietly to a Cuban prison. There I could be beaten and tortured, then 'disappear.' Only my aunt Ana would ask about me, and she would be ignored."

I gasped. "You'd be killed?"

"There is an alternative—what they have done to some escapees who have been returned. My work in baseball would be discredited in the press, and I would no longer be allowed to play. I'd be assigned a low-paying, menial job."

"What about the people who know you—your friends, your teachers? Wouldn't they come forward to help you?"

Shaking his head, Ricky said, "Rose, there is a big difference between a democracy and a dictatorship. In Cuba you survive by *not* asking questions or offering help."

"What are you doing on this ship?" I asked. "Don't most of the people who escape Cuba try to take boats directly to Miami?"

"Yes," Ricky said. "And with your coast guard on constant patrol, they are usually caught. By the laws your country established, those who set foot on your land may ask for political asylum. Those who are picked up at sea must be returned to Cuba. I must do all that I can to reach United States soil so that I can request asylum. I cannot, I *cannot* go back."

I didn't answer. I patiently waited for Ricky to get a grip on his feelings.

Finally he said, "I left Cuba, thanks to my uncle Martín. He made the plans. It was his idea for me to travel south, in the opposite direction from Miami, where air patrols would not be looking for escapees. With the help of his friends and Tía Ana's friends, Uncle Martín hired the owner of a small fishing boat and instructed him to take me to people he knew about in Haiti. I joined some of those who were hired by the cruise line to work on Bonita Beach, where I hid until my uncle arrived. He brought me the clothes I have on and my I.D. card. He has other clothing for me in our stateroom."

I spoke my thoughts aloud. "He paid your passage, and he hired someone your age to board the ship in order to get an identification card for you." I looked up. "But what about your birth certificate or a passport? If they're under your assumed name, they must be forged."

Ricky shrugged. "Where Uncle Martín got the official papers needed, I do not know. That is his business, not mine."

"What will happen if you get to Miami?"

Shuddering, Ricky whispered, "Not *if*. *When* I get to Miami, there will be friends of my uncle there to meet the ship. They will have a job for me with their ball club, and they will help me as I ask for political asylum."

"You're a baseball player?"

"Yes. Like my uncle Martín." He shifted, rocking the bed. "I do not understand how the Cuban authorities suspected I would be on this ship," he said. His voice dropped, as though he were talking to himself.

"My grandmother might have notified the *policía* that I was missing, but she would have done it out of concern. She would not have wanted me to come to harm. Since her university days in the fifties, she has been a strong, unyielding supporter of Fidel Castro, but I am her grandson."

"Did your uncle Martín defect from Cuba?"

"Yes."

"What did your grandmother do then?"

Ricky paused, staring down at the floor before he quietly answered, "When Uncle Martín left Cuba for the freedom of the United States, Abuela Beatriz denounced her brother-in-law as a traitor. She has not spoken his name since."

Sighing, Ricky added, "You must not blame my grandmother for what she thinks. Our news media is controlled so that we see and hear only what government officials want us to know. Everything must be under the control of the state. The police have too much authority, and many people live in fear, but my grandmother stubbornly defends Castro and his regime. She—and many others—despised life under the dictator Fulgencio Batista and counted on Castro to better everyone's living conditions. Instead, conditions under communism became worse. This is hard for those who favor communism to accept."

Ricky's face showed his misery as he said, "I am afraid my grandmother will have the same hatred toward me for defying the cause for which she

71

risked her life." He threw a quick glance at me. "You may think her stubborn, but it is a cause she believes in, one for which she has taken a stand. I do not expect you to *comprende.*"

In a way I *did* understand. "Always stand up for what you believe in," Mom kept telling me. That was what Ricky's grandmother had done. But what if people changed and dreams became twisted? I shook my head, trying to shoo the questions away. They made my head hurt because I didn't have answers.

Ricky got to his feet and paced to the sliding glass doors that opened onto the balcony. "If Abuela Beatriz reported to the authorities that I was missing, they would be looking for me. But why would they look toward Haiti and not Miami? There is a possibility, of course, that the boatman broke his promise of secrecy. Either he was caught returning to Cuba or he volunteered information, hoping to be rewarded."

He thought a moment, then said, "I followed directions. What could have gone wrong? I don't know what to do next. I can't go to Uncle Martín's stateroom. That is the first place they will look. Then they'll search all the places on the ship where someone could hide."

I glanced at my watch. "Glory's going to come back to our stateroom soon. The bridge players will want to dress for dinner." I sucked in a sharp breath as an idea popped into my mind. "If they search the ship and don't find you, then they'll decide they were wrong and you can't be aboard. Right? So we'll hide you—as least until after the ship sails. I think I know where you'll be safe."

As I reached for the telephone, Ricky moved quickly, clamping a hand over mine. His eyes had narrowed, and his breath came in shallow bursts. "Who are you calling?" he demanded.

"I know you're afraid, but you came to me for help, and I'm going to help you," I told him. "You'll have to trust me."

For a moment Ricky didn't move or speak. I didn't either. I could only wait for what he would say. Finally he pulled his hand away, his chin jutting out stubbornly. "I am *not* afraid," he said. "I just don't know whom to trust."

"You can trust me," I said again. I glanced at my watch again. *Don't come yet, Glory,* I thought. *Give us a few more minutes.* I quickly dialed Neil's room number. As soon as he answered I said, "We've got a problem. I need your help right away."

"Where are you?" Neil asked.

"In my stateroom."

"I'll be right there," he said.

I hung up the phone, grateful to Neil for not wasting time asking questions.

When he arrived a few minutes later, his hair still damp from his shower, I motioned him to the small sofa. Then I said to Ricky, "You can trust both of us. I promise. Tell Neil what you told me. He's going to help you."

"I am?" Neil asked in surprise.

"Just listen," I said. I sat on the sofa next to him.

"My name is Enrique Urbino," Ricky said to Neil. "And you were right. My uncle is Martín Urbino, who was once a shortstop for the Havana Sugar Kings in Cuba. When he signed with the Cincinnati Reds in 1960, defecting to the United States, he was listed as a traitor to Cuba."

Neil leaned forward eagerly. "Your uncle was one of many baseball players who left Cuba to join teams in the United States. Like Bert Campanaris, Tony Perez, Francisco—"

I put a hand on Neil's arm. "Just listen," I said. "We can talk baseball later."

But Ricky was carried away, probably glad to talk about something familiar and safe. He told Neil, "The game of baseball is Cuba's passion. Fidel Castro has always supported the league with his presence. Children are watched for signs of talent and promise in the game, and some are chosen to be enrolled at the special baseball academies for elementary school students."

"Were you?" Neil interrupted.

"Yes," Ricky said. "I have played with youth teams and then the minor league. Last year I was assigned to the Habana Leones, the top team in the Cuban league."

Neil whistled. "What's your position? Your batting average? Are you left-handed, like your uncle?"

"Neil!" I demanded. "Let Ricky tell his story."

Voices rumbled in the passageway. For a moment they paused just outside the door and we all froze. We heard another stateroom door open, then close, and the voices moved on.

Ricky let out the breath he'd been holding, then told Neil and me about his nighttime trip from Cuba to Haiti. He slumped, adding, "Recently, I was publicly honored by Fidel. To leave Cuba after receiving this honor is not only treason but—in Fidel's opinion—a terrible personal insult, embarrassing him in the eyes of the world."

"Have you tried before to leave Cuba?" Neil asked.

"No," Ricky answered.

"What about when your team played in other countries, like Venezuela? Or in the Atlanta Olympics, or the International World Cup? Couldn't you have just walked out of your hotel and into an American embassy?"

Ricky's mouth twisted. "I have not played for the Cuban National team in the United States. I have been allowed to play only in Central and South American countries. When we traveled, we did not stay in dormitories or hotels, as teams from other countries do. Cots were set up for us in the basement rooms of the stadiums. We slept and ate there under guard. We never left the stadiums until it was time for us to board the planes to fly back to Cuba."

Neil thought a moment before he spoke. "Just a short time ago, two of your Cuban ballplayers asked the United States for political asylum. Rigoberto Herrera Betancourt, one of your pitching coaches, disappeared in Baltimore while the Cuban National team was on the way to the airport after winning over the Orioles. He showed up at a police station and asked for political asylum. He was offered a job with Madison's Black Wolf team."

"He had help," Ricky said quietly. "Like the help Uncle Martín is getting for me."

Neil looked serious. "The other one was Andy Morales. He was sent back."

Ricky shivered, rubbing his upper arms as if he were cold. "He tried to escape by boat with around thirty other people. The boat ran out of fuel twenty-five miles from the Florida Keys, and the United States Coast Guard intercepted them. The Immigration and Naturalization Service sent all of them back to Cuba. That is the rule. If you're picked up at sea, you're sent back. If you set foot on U.S. soil, you can ask for asylum."

My heart gave a jump as I thought of what it would be like to be sent back to Cuba. "What happened to Andy Morales?" I asked.

"It was announced that he had decided to quit baseball, since he was overrated as a player, and had chosen instead to work for the Cuban National Sports Institute, overseeing sports programs," Ricky said.

"Oh, well, if he was overrated—" I began, but Ricky interrupted.

"That is not true. That is what the government announced. That is what the press reported. Anyone who tries to escape Cuba is publicly discredited. I know Andy. I know how he loves baseball and what a good player he is. And I do not believe giving it up was his choice."

I looked at my watch again. It was five minutes to four. The ship was supposed to leave the harbor at four. Glory would be here soon to change for dinner. I had to break into the conversation.

"Neil, someone from Cuba is on this ship searching for Ricky," I said. "We can't let them find him. You said that your stateroom was connected to your grandmother's but separate. Could he share your stateroom for a while? Can you keep him hidden?"

"Yes," Neil said. He turned to Ricky. "We can stop off at your uncle's stateroom and get your clothes."

"That would not be wise!" Ricky exclaimed. "The stateroom may be watched."

Neil shrugged. "We're about the same size. You can borrow some of my clothes for now." A smile flickered on his face as he said to me, "Except for my Hawaiian shirts."

"Will there be any problem with your grandmother?" I asked Neil. "Is there any chance she'll discover Ricky?"

"None," Neil said. "Grandma is hard of hearing and has poor eyesight. Besides, she always knocks and waits for me to open the door to my room. We won't have trouble keeping her from knowing Ricky is there. He'll have time to duck into the bathroom to hide."

The jangle of the telephone made me jump. As I reached for the receiver I realized my hands were shaking. "Y-yes?" I asked.

"Rosie," Glory said, "at least I found *you*. Do you have any idea where Neil is?"

"He's here," I answered, quickly adding, "There's a bunch of us here."

"Well, I'm in Eloise's stateroom," Glory told me. "I helped her dress for dinner. Tell Neil to come on up. I've got to leave Eloise to get dressed myself."

"I'll tell him," I said. As I hung up the phone, I relayed the message.

Neil strode to the door, but Ricky hung back. As he pulled his straw hat down over his face, he couldn't seem to keep his hands from trembling. "*Por favor,* check the passageway first," he whispered. "Is anyone out there?"

Opening the door, Neil stepped out of the stateroom, looking to both sides. "All clear," he said.

To my surprise, Ricky took my hands and lightly kissed my cheek. I felt his breath warm against my ear. "Thank you, Rose," he murmured.

Even if I'd found the words to answer him, I didn't have the chance. Ricky slipped through the door, shutting it behind him.

I backed up, sitting on one of the twin beds. The salt-and-sun fragrance of Ricky's skin was still with me, and I liked it.

Within a few minutes Glory burst into the stateroom and stopped short, staring at me. "You're still in your bathing suit? You haven't dressed yet? Well, I suppose we'll fight over who gets the shower first. What in the world have you been doing, Rosie?"

How was I supposed to answer that question truthfully? I could hardly say "I was helping to hide a political escapee." Trying to change the subject, I asked, "How did your bridge game go?"

"My partner and I are scoring high," Glory said smugly. "If we keep getting dealt hands like the ones we've been getting, we're going to win some big prizes."

She grinned mischievously. "One thing about your grandmother, Rosie. I may be growing older faster than I'd like to, but I still have plenty of energy—more than *some* people in our bridge group. Alice and Myrna have cratered. They said they'd never make it to the dining room and are going to have room service."

"You're not getting old, Glory," I began, but Glory didn't seem to expect an answer. She had already found her shower cap and cosmetics bag and was heading for the bathroom.

As I walked to the chest of drawers to get my own things, I felt the movement of the ship. We were setting sail. I changed direction, sliding open the glass door to the balcony, and stepped outside. Haiti was rapidly turning into a shrinking blur of deep green mist, and a small powerboat was leaving the ship, bouncing up and down in the wake.

I leaned over the rail and stared, trying to make out the three figures in the boat. Was one of them wearing a khaki uniform? From this distance it appeared so, but it was hard to tell. If the military officer from Cuba had left the ship, then he had stopped looking for Ricky. I straightened, breathing a long sigh of relief. Ricky would be safe.

"Your turn!" Glory called, and I hurried back into the stateroom to shower and dress.

I wondered how I could find out if the officer from Cuba had given up the search for Ricky. I hadn't been able to see the figures in the boat clearly. What if my guess was wrong and the officer was still on board? Would Mr. Diago—Mr. Urbino—know? Could I ask him? Or would it be better to pretend I knew nothing of Ricky's attempt to escape?

What should I do?

I didn't have a clue what my next move should be. But as my mind drifted back to my conversation with Ricky and the warm feeling it gave me when he called me Rose, I did make one decision. I might just change my name.

As I STEPPED OUT OF THE ELEVATOR, TRAILING FAR behind Glory, Julieta suddenly appeared. She looked at me accusingly. "You said you'd meet me. None of you came."

I gulped and took a step backward. "Oh, no," I said without thinking. "With all that was happening, I forgot."

Julieta's eyes narrowed as she stared at me suspiciously. "What was happening?"

I fumbled for an answer. There was no way I could tell her about Ricky. "Well, we got to talking, and then Glory called from the Flemings' stateroom and said that Neil's grandmother needed him, and then I had to get ready for dinner, and . . . well, I forgot we had said we'd meet you."

Julieta turned away, the hurt she was feeling clouding her eyes.

I put a hand on her arm. "Look, Julieta, I'm really sorry. There's a problem we had to solve, and I was a little scared . . . well, worried. I'm still not sure what to do."

"What problem?" Her look changed to one of open curiosity.

"I can't . . . that is, it's a personal problem."

"You can tell me."

"No, I can't."

Julieta's eyes sparked, and she gave a little snicker. "I'll find out sooner or later. If there's something I really want to know, nothing can keep me from finding out."

I was astonished. "I'd tell you if I could, but—"

Neil's arrival with his grandmother stopped me from blurting out what I really wanted to say— that Julieta had no business being so nosy. Neil bent over his grandmother as he introduced her to Julieta.

Mrs. Fleming, peering intently at both of us, mixed us up. She graciously told me she was happy to meet me and told Julieta she hoped she'd enjoyed the snorkeling trip as much as Neil had.

Julieta rested her long fingers on Neil's arm. "I wish we were at the same dinner seating," she said, pouting. "But we're not. Why don't we meet at ten at Star Struck? They're going to have a kara-oke contest."

"I'm sorry," Neil said. "This has been a long day, and I'm beat. I'm going to spend the evening with Grandma."

Julieta looked at me with a challenge in her eyes. "I suppose you'll be with your friend Ricky," she said.

"No, I won't," I said quickly. "I don't know what Ricky will be doing."

"Then come with me to Star Struck. Ten o'clock." She looked as friendly as when I'd first met her.

I hesitated. I would have liked to go to Star Struck to find out what the other kids on the ship were doing and dance to some good music, but I wanted to be available in case Ricky needed me. "We'll be docking in Jamaica tomorrow morning. How about going sightseeing together?" I asked Julieta. "Or will you be with your parents?"

She brightened. "They won't care what I do. Want to sign up for the tour group that's climbing the Dunn's River Falls?"

"I'd love to."

Mrs. Fleming twisted in her wheelchair to look up at Neil. "When are we going into the dining room? I'm getting hungry," she said.

"Right now, Grandma," Neil answered.

"See you later," I said to Julieta. Glory had already entered the dining room, so I walked beside Neil as we headed toward our table.

84

Quietly, so only I could hear, Neil said, "I ordered room service for him. I told him to sign my name."

I looked up, surprised. "Thanks," I said. Guiltily, I realized that I hadn't thought about feeding Ricky.

"A boat left the ship just before we sailed from Bonita Beach," I told Neil. "I think that military officer was on it."

Neil gave a shrug. "And maybe he wasn't. Ricky phoned his uncle's stateroom. His uncle told him to stay where he was. The uncle doesn't trust anyone."

"Neither does Ricky," I said.

"He doesn't like being cooped up in our stateroom," Neil said. "He's sure that the search for him was called off once the ship set sail. But I made him promise to stay there while we were at dinner."

Neil came to a stop at our table and turned to give me a strange, almost yearning look I didn't understand. "I think he trusts you, Rosie," he said.

I took a deep breath and heard myself saying, "Neil, I'm too old to be called Rosie. From now on will you call me Rose?"

"Sure," Neil said. "Rose."

I winced. It didn't sound the same as when Ricky spoke my name.

Neil busied himself making his grandmother comfortable. Then he sat next to me. "Your new friend wants you to call the stateroom when dinner is over," he said, then turned to Mrs. Duncastle to continue their discussion about baseball.

During dinner, with the wonderful food and the golden staircase and the glittering chandeliers, I felt guilty about Mom. Mom loved shrimp cocktail. Mom's favorite show tunes were included in a piano medley. Why hadn't I made peace with her before I left on the trip?

Right after dinner I went to the ship's library, where a sign on the desk listed the e-mail rate as fifty cents a minute. I had some spending money. I could pay Glory back.

Dear Mom, I typed. *I miss you. You don't always think I want to talk to you, but I really do, and I would if you'd give me the chance. Glory listens, but you . . .*

I deleted everything back to *I miss you* and started over. I wanted to tell her about Ricky, but how did I know who else would read this e-mail? Hadn't there been lots of stories in the news about e-mail not really being private? I couldn't write about Ricky.

Dear Mom, I miss you. You'd love this ship, and I keep thinking how I wish you were here. Someday maybe you and I can take a cruise together. I hope so. I love you, Rose Ann.

I clicked *Send* and *OK*.

I flopped back in the chair, disappointed. I hadn't said any of the things I really wanted to say. I hadn't written anything that would make up for the argument Mom and I'd had. When I saw how much time it had taken me to write an e-mail that added up to the same old "wish you were here," I was shocked. At fifty cents a minute?

It was close to eight o'clock by my watch, so I went to the stateroom and telephoned Ricky. Glory and some of her friends had gone to the lounge to see the evening's entertainment. I was eager to talk to Ricky, even if it was only for a few moments.

I expected Neil to answer the phone, but instead I heard Ricky's voice.

"I want to see you, Rose," he said.

"That might not be a good idea," I told him. "We don't want to disturb Neil's grandmother."

"I didn't mean here," Ricky said. "Can we find a quiet place on the ship?"

"There are no quiet places on this ship," I cautioned. "For your own safety, you should stay where you are."

"The sunbathing deck should be deserted. Meet me by the forward elevators on deck twelve in five minutes. And wear a sweater. Night winds off the ocean can be chilly."

"Someone might see you in the elevator."

"I will take care not to be seen," Ricky answered.

"You're taking a chance, Ricky. . . . Ricky?" But he had hung up the phone.

I shivered as I put down the receiver. I pulled on a light sweater and hurried from our stateroom. All I could do was try to convince Ricky to return to Mrs. Fleming's suite and stay there until we knew for sure he was safe. I was frightened, but at the same time I was deliriously happy that he wanted to be with me. The feelings didn't mix well.

Rounding a corner, I nearly bumped into Tommy, the cruise director, who was pacing in front of the elevator bank. As he jabbed at the button, a woman laughed and said, "That won't make it come any sooner."

"I don't have much time. I've got to find a few minutes of peace and quiet," he complained.

The woman glanced at me. Tommy did too, but he went back to what he was saying as if I weren't there. Plenty of people were like that, I thought. If you were a kid you were nonexistent. You couldn't see, hear, or think. I hadn't liked Tommy Jansen when I first saw him on deck, and now I liked him even less.

Tommy glanced at his watch and said to the woman, "I have to be back to close the first show in an hour and then get ready for the second show." He let out a sigh and added, "They didn't tell me I'd be on with this charming and smiling stuff twenty-four hours around the clock."

"I know," the woman said, "or you wouldn't have taken the job." She rolled her eyes as if she'd heard his story over and over again.

Tommy shrugged and grinned sheepishly. "Okay, okay," he said. "I took it because I was broke and badly needed the money. You don't know anybody who's got a few thousand dollars he doesn't know what to do with, do you?"

"Oh, sure," the woman said. "Lots of people."

One of the elevator bells dinged, the doors opened, and the two of them stepped in. I stayed where I was. I didn't like being ignored, and I didn't want to hear any more of Tommy's complaining. As soon as their elevator left, I pressed the Up button, and in just a few seconds another elevator arrived—an empty elevator, I was glad to see.

When I stepped out onto deck twelve, there was no sign of Ricky. Aft on the deck, past the swimming pools, I could see tiny figures silhouetted in the golden glare of a sweep of bright windows, creatures in another world, far away and soundless. I walked from the light of the elevator area into the darkness near the rail. Ricky had been right. The night wind was chilly, and I shivered.

"Rose."

Ricky took my hand and led me through an open doorway into the dimness of the prow. But suddenly I stopped, alert to the sound of footsteps behind us.

"Someone else is on deck with us. Wait here," I

whispered to Ricky. I retraced my steps to the pool of bright light at the elevator doors. The footsteps ahead of me quickened. I heard the ding of an elevator and the doors opening. When I reached the elevator, it had already left, and the area was empty.

Ricky stepped up beside me. "Don't look so worried," he said. "Someone was just enjoying the night air. Or maybe he lost his way. If he had been looking for me, he wouldn't leave just when he found me."

"I guess you're right," I said. Reassured, I strolled the darkened deck with Ricky, putting the incident out of my mind. Ricky had asked me to meet him, and I wasn't about to spoil our time together by jumping at every little sound. The darkness pulled the stars down, magnifying their brightness, and Ricky's hand in mine was warm and comforting.

We found two deck chairs tucked into an inside nook, out of the wind. Ricky pushed them together; we sat down, and he took my hand again. "Tell me about yourself," he said. "You're the person who is so kind to help me."

"There's nothing to tell," I answered. "There's just Mom and me . . . and Glory, my grandmother."

Ricky studied my face. "There must be much more to tell about yourself. You go to school, don't you? What do you study?"

Looking into his eyes, with his handsome face so close, I couldn't think. "N-nothing special. I—I just take the regular classes everyone else takes," I said.

"I think you must be the most popular girl in school. Am I right?" He smiled.

"Not exactly." Miserable at the sudden memory of Cam's dumping me at Cassie's party and the police coming and Mom so angry, I tried to change the subject. "Tell me about Cuba," I said.

"It is a beautiful island," he answered, "but why should we talk about Cuba? I want to know more about *you*."

"Why?" I asked.

Ricky didn't answer. He turned on his left side so that he was even closer to me. He put a hand behind my shoulders, drawing me closer, and his lips met mine.

"Does that answer your question?" he asked, and I opened my eyes, trying to make myself believe that I was back on Earth.

"If we stood in the prow of the ship," I whispered in a trembling voice, "and if you held me while I stretched out my arms . . ."

Ricky glanced ahead at the prow, gleaming white in the moonlight. "It is off limits," he said. "See the barriers?"

I nodded as reality caught up to me with a

thump. Discarding the romantic dreamworld Becca had put into my mind, I said, "You and I are also off limits. We have just five days left until the ship docks in the United States, and then—"

"The United States," Ricky echoed. I could see that the yearning in his eyes was not for me.

"Ricky," I asked, "if your request for political asylum is granted when you reach the United States, where will you go?"

"To a team in the minor leagues," he said. "In one of your northern states."

I shivered. "I'll go back to west Texas. We'll be well over a thousand miles apart."

"Don't think about what will happen," Ricky said. "Think only about the present." Before I could react, he pulled me close and kissed me again.

We were interrupted by sudden footsteps and a flash of light so bright that I threw an arm across my eyes, squinting upward.

Ricky was pulled to his feet by two large crew members, and I scrambled up too. "What's going on?" I cried to the ship's officer who stood before us.

The officer gave me only a brief glance before he turned to Ricky. "Enrique Urbino, I am John Wilson, chief of security on this ship. By order of the captain, I am placing you under arrest."

"No! You can't!" I insisted. "His uncle paid his

fare. He has the same rights as any other passenger on this ship."

The officer looked at me so sternly that I shivered. "Not in this case," he said. "Mr. Urbino has been charged by the Cuban government with the crime of murder."

I RAN AFTER THE MEN WHO WERE TAKING RICKY. "WAIT for me!" I shouted, and pushed behind them through the door to the private stairway leading to the captain's office behind the bridge.

Mr. Wilson didn't try to stop me. He simply ignored me as he led the way through another series of doors and passages, finally stopping to knock at a wide paneled door.

"Come in," a deep voice called. The door opened, and again I squeezed ahead to be with Ricky before it was shut.

Captain Helmut Olson stood behind a large desk of dark, polished wood. With a few painted landscapes on the walls and framed photos on the desk, the office looked more like that of a businessman on shore than a captain on a ship. But I didn't have time to think about where I was.

Scowling, Captain Olson studied Ricky. "Mr. Urbino, you will be confined to the brig until we dock in Miami on Sunday morning. There you'll be turned over to the INS. Their agents will return you to Cuba."

Ricky stood tall, meeting the captain's gaze, but his face was pale. "These men said I killed someone. I did not kill anyone. Whoever told you this is lying."

The man in the Cuban military uniform, who had been out of our line of vision, suddenly stepped from the corner of the office, startling me. I gasped, recognizing him.

"I am Major Carlos Cepeda," he said to Ricky. "I do not lie. A man has been murdered." He tossed two photographs on the desk—his large gold initial ring gleaming—and leaned into Ricky's face. "Here is the proof."

I didn't have a chance to shield my gaze from the photographs, and I shuddered violently when I saw them. They were photos of a man's lifeless face. He was bruised and bloody and looked as if he'd been beaten to death.

Ricky cried out, "Raúl! The boatman!"

"Exactly," Major Cepeda said. "The fisherman who helped you escape. You killed him to keep him from reporting your flight from Cuba."

"I did not kill him," Ricky insisted. "He helped me. I would have done nothing to harm him."

"We have witnesses from a *cantina* near the town of Morón. They saw you beat the fisherman, kill him, and try to sink the boat before you left. Unfortunately for you, the boat remained afloat, so the witnesses could pull it ashore."

"No!" Ricky insisted. "You are wrong! You are lying!"

Something definitely didn't sound right about all this. I took a step forward. "Where was the boat found?" I asked the major.

Captain Olson answered instead. "Ms. Marstead, you were allowed to accompany Mr. Urbino to my office because we have questions to ask you about your part in helping Mr. Urbino hide out on this ship. However, you have no part in *this* investigation, so I ask you to remain silent." He gestured to a grouping of chairs at the far side of the large office. "You may be seated, if you wish."

My heart began to beat so loudly I could hear it, and I had to swallow twice before I could talk, but I took another step forward and said, "Please, sir, answer this one question."

"It has no bearing on the charge," the captain said.

"Please!" I insisted.

Major Cepeda's lips twisted in a mirthless smile. "It is of no matter, but if it will silence this persistent young woman, I shall tell her. The boat was wedged under a small pier which is located near Morón."

"In Cuba?"

"Of course."

I turned to Captain Olson. "There is your proof that Ricky—Enrique—couldn't have committed the murder. The boatman took him to Haiti and left him there. Enrique had no other transportation. He couldn't possibly have followed the boatman back to Cuba and killed him. And even if in some weird way he had, then how would he have returned to Haiti in time to be taken to Bonita Beach to meet his uncle and board your ship?"

The captain's only reaction was a blink of surprise before he turned to the officer. "Major Cepeda, how do you answer this?"

The major slid his large gold ring up and down his finger nervously. "There—there were witnesses," he stammered.

"Who are lying for you," Ricky said.

"Ms. Marstead's logistics seem to be correct," Captain Olson said. "If Mr. Urbino planned to kill the boatman, he would have accomplished this in Haiti. There would have been no purpose or time to return to Cuba, then travel back to Haiti."

Major Cepeda's chin jutted out stubbornly, and he blustered, "This is a matter for the Cuban courts to decide when Enrique Urbino is back in our country, where the crime took place. My office offered a reward for his capture. Ten thousand

American dollars. You saw the flyers. I took it upon myself to leave copies of the flyers in the public areas of the ship."

It was clear that Captain Olson didn't like to have his authority challenged. "You shouldn't have done that without my permission," he snapped. "The reward is offered for the capture of a murderer, and it's obvious from what you have told us that Enrique Urbino is not a murderer."

Major Cepeda kept sliding his ring up and down his finger. A part of my mind kept thinking, *If his ring is that loose, he's going to lose it.* But I focused on what he was saying. "The reward is to be given for the return of Enrique Urbino to Cuba. I will take command of the prisoner and make arrangements to return with him to Cuba when we dock in Jamaica tomorrow."

You can't do that! I wanted to cry, but I knew I'd better keep quiet. I looked to the captain for help and tensed, sucking in my breath.

Captain Olson's eyes had narrowed, and his voice was cold as he said, "Major Cepeda, this is my ship, and I am in command. I intend to keep Mr. Urbino in my custody until we dock in Miami. There he will be turned over to the Immigration and Naturalization Service, as is proper. Tomorrow, as soon as we dock in Ocho Rios, you will leave the ship, and Mr. Urbino will remain aboard."

"But if he escapes—"

"Mr. Urbino will not have the opportunity to escape."

"You will confine him to the brig?"

"There is no need for that. He will be confined to his stateroom while we are in port. While we are at sea, he will be given the run of the ship. I assure you that upon our arrival in Miami, he will be turned over to the INS. They will have the responsibility of returning him to Cuba."

"Why?" I blurted out. "He's innocent of any crime."

Still formal and still intimidating, Captain Olson said, "You are excused, Major Cepeda."

The captain was silent as the major, stiff with anger, strode from his office. Then he dismissed the two men who had aided his security chief, Officer Wilson. As Captain Olson turned his black gaze on me, I moved closer to Ricky. I was frightened at having spoken out, but there was more I needed to say.

"The Cuban officer lied," I insisted. "It wasn't even a well-thought-out lie, because it made no sense." I deliberately forced myself to glance down at the photographs of the boatman's badly beaten face, and for the first time I noticed the small C-shaped cuts on his left cheek and forehead. Again I shuddered.

"There are laws of the sea as well as laws of the land we must obey," Captain Olson told me. "I intend to follow the correct procedure."

"But Ricky is innocent," I said again.

"Perhaps innocent of the crime of murder, but Mr. Urbino is not innocent of traveling under an assumed name with a forged passport."

"His fare was paid. In full. By his uncle."

"That is of no consequence."

"What will happen to my uncle Martín?" Ricky suddenly asked, and I could hear the worry in his voice.

"Nothing, as far as we are concerned," the captain said. "Although he seems to have introduced himself to a few passengers aboard ship as José Diago, he registered for the voyage under his rightful name and he carries the proper identification and passport. As for the forged passport he supposedly obtained for you, that is something he will have to take up with officials within the United States. It is not my immediate concern."

Captain Olson gestured to the chairs again. "Let us all be seated. We will begin by discussing Mr. Enrique Urbino's position with him. You asked for the truth, Mr. Urbino. Now I am asking *you* for the truth. Please tell me how you came aboard my ship and where you have been hiding."

I sat quietly and uncomfortably between Officer Wilson and the captain while Ricky repeated everything he had told me about his flight to Haiti, his method of boarding the ship, and his short stay in the Flemings' stateroom.

Captain Olson thought a few moments before answering. Finally he said, "Under the circumstances, I think we can dismiss any wrongdoing on the part of Mrs. Fleming and her grandson." His eyes drilled into mine as he added, "And I suppose on your part, Ms. Marstead."

I gave a huge sigh of relief, slumping in my chair. "Thank you, Captain," I said. "And Ricky, too?"

"Mr. Urbino is not included. As I mentioned, he is aboard under false and illegal pretenses and will be delivered to officials from the INS as soon as we dock in Miami."

As Captain Olson stood, he said, "Mr. Urbino, I will send Officer Wilson to accompany you to your uncle's stateroom. Since we will dock in Jamaica early tomorrow morning, Officer Wilson will arrange for a guard to be posted outside your door, beginning immediately. Tomorrow your breakfast and lunch will be delivered to you. After we sail at six P.M., you will once again be free to roam the ship. We will repeat the procedure on Friday while we are docked in Cozumel."

Ricky slowly got to his feet, and I stood, too. I felt strange in the presence of this formal, unyielding captain. Automatically I said, "Thank you, sir," but my mind was desperately searching for some idea that could help Ricky. I couldn't let him be turned over to the INS to be returned to Cuba. There had to be a way for him to reach United States soil so he could ask for asylum. If I thought enough and hoped enough, maybe I could come up with something.

In spite of Officer Wilson, who stood close beside Ricky at the elevator, Ricky wrapped his arms around me in a quick hug. "Thank you for standing by me," he said.

I tried to smile. "When the captain had time to think about what Major Cepeda had said, he would have figured out that you couldn't have committed the murder," I said. "He didn't really need me to point it out."

The security chief nodded. "It was obvious to all of us," he agreed.

The elevator signal dinged, and I began to step back, but Ricky held me even more tightly, burying his face in my hair. With his lips close to my ear he whispered, "I can't go back to Cuba."

I could only nod. He was asking me for help, but we were up against the captain and his staff and the rules he had to follow. At the moment I couldn't think of a single thing I could do that would help Ricky.

As the elevator doors opened, Officer Wilson stepped forward, one hand on Ricky's shoulder.

"I'll see you tomorrow night," I told Ricky. I tried to sound positive, but as the doors closed between us I shivered, sharing Ricky's fear.

I went to deck five. Major Cepeda had said he'd put the flyers in public places. The lounges around the main desk would probably have been his first choice. I suspected that the captain would send someone to gather up the flyers and toss them, and I wanted to be sure to get one, to read exactly what Ricky was charged with.

It was getting late, and the lounges were nearly deserted. The passengers who were still partying were most likely in the ballroom. I could hear the faint sounds of a trumpet and the rhythm of drum-beats—slow and steady, for people who were winding down.

A few scattered sheets of paper lay on one of the round tables near the windows, and two people were standing by the table reading from one of the sheets. One was one of the security assistants I had seen in the captain's office. The other was the cruise director, Tommy Jansen.

I waited, stepping sideways so I was behind a potted tree. I didn't want to interrupt their conversation.

"I could use that ten thousand," Mr. Jansen said.

The security assistant chuckled. "It sounds good, but there's no way of collecting it."

Mr. Jansen turned to look at him. "Why not? The kid just has to be delivered back to Cuba."

"That's all? And how would you go about doing that?"

There was silence for a moment; then Mr. Jansen said, "I'd have to give it some thought, but it could be done—maybe when the ship reaches Mexico."

"The captain put him under guard. He's going through legal channels. He won't even let that

Cuban major have him. I bet the major will be ordered off the ship once we reach Jamaica."

"All to the good," Mr. Jansen said. "I'm beginning to get an idea, and it's gonna work better with the major out of the way."

He folded the flyer he was holding and stuck it in his pocket as they left the lounge. I ran to the table and picked up the half dozen or so that were left. I headed for the elevator, suddenly afraid of the lonely silence and the creepy wail of the trumpet that shivered through the empty lounge.

A few minutes later, I stepped off the elevator and found a guard sitting outside Ricky's room. I nodded and quietly entered the stateroom I shared with Glory, hoping she was too sound asleep to be disturbed. But she was seated in robe and slippers on the small sofa with an open book in her hands. "Did you and Neil go to that teen hangout?" she asked. "Did you have a good time?"

"You didn't need to wait up for me," I said, trying to sidestep the answer.

Glory smiled. "Old habits," she said. "I used to wait for your father to come home when he was a teenager. And maybe I feel a special responsibility for you because you're my only grandchild."

As she closed her book and laid it aside, I realized I didn't have to answer her questions. But that wasn't right. I had always been honest with her, and it was important that this honesty continue.

"Glory," I said, as I sat beside her, "I need to talk to you."

I showed her the flyers and told her about Ricky and his arrest.

Glory shuddered when I told her about the photographs of the murdered boatman. "A man was murdered?" she whispered.

"Major Cepeda insisted that Ricky did it."

"Rosie, who is this boy?"

I took Glory's hand, concerned that she was pale and there was fear in her eyes. "Ricky didn't do it," I insisted. "The captain and security chief believe he's innocent too. I'll tell you why."

And I did, describing all that had taken place in the captain's office.

By the time I finished the story, Glory's face had regained its color, but she shook her head as if unwilling to believe that had happened. "Your mother was worried about a simple party that went bad. Now you're involved in hiding a fugitive from murder?"

"I told you, Ricky didn't murder that boatman," I said.

"I know. You made that perfectly clear." Glory scowled. "That was a stupid trick the Cuban officer pulled. He must be pretty arrogant to think he could get away with that." She took one of the flyers from my hand and studied it. Finally, she said, "Don't worry about this reward offered for

Ricky's return. Even if someone wants the money, he's not likely to try to spirit Ricky off to Cuba to collect it. Can you imagine Dora Duncastle and Winnie Applebee wrestling Ricky away from the guard at his door, then carrying him off the ship and onto a plane waiting to fly him to Cuba?"

"No, I can't," I answered, but from what I'd overheard Tommy Jansen saying, there was at least one person on board who might try it.

"So don't worry," Glory said, looking self-satisfied. "Fifty percent of the passengers on this ship are not in any kind of physical condition to attempt an abduction, and ninety-nine percent couldn't care less about aiding the Cuban government."

"But I heard the cruise director talking about getting the reward," I said.

"Did he say how he was going to manage it?"

"He said he was working on an idea."

Glory patted my shoulder. "As a stand-up comic, he's mildly funny. As a cruise director, I suppose he's okay. But beyond that—" She chuckled and said, "If I were Ricky, I wouldn't worry. Now, if you want my legal advice . . ."

"I do."

"According to what you told me, Ricky is underage and will be for the next two months. You said his grandmother had raised him?"

"It was really his great-aunt Ana."

"Legally, it was his grandmother. Let's not get

sidetracked. She can demand that Ricky be sent back, since he is a minor in her care."

"But what if he sets foot on United States soil—not as a prisoner of the INS, but as a political escapee?"

"Even so, it will be up to the INS to decide his future. Of course, the uncle could take their decision to court." She thought for a moment, then said, "From what you told me, the captain of our ship has made the right decision."

She walked to the door and peered through the peephole. Then she came back to where I was seated. "The guard is there," she said. "I was going to offer him a chair, but he has one."

I was still devastated by what she had told me. "Glory, Ricky needs help. This is no time to worry about getting somebody a chair."

Glory rested a hand on my shoulder. "Stop worrying about that baseball player. He'll be safe while he's on the ship. And if you need my help for anything, I hope you know I'm here for you."

"Thanks, Glory. But when we get back to Miami—"

"As the captain told you, everything will be handled by the INS." She yawned and said, "Right now, it's past time for bed, and tomorrow we're signed up for an early trip to Dunn's River Falls."

"Oh!" I said. "I thought you'd be playing bridge, so I told Julieta I'd go with her."

"No problem. She's on the same list we are. So

is Neil, who is really a very fine young man, if you'd just pay attention. I'm sure if you gave him even half a chance, you and he could hit it off."

"Glory," I said, wishing she didn't have such a one-track mind, "Neil is a nice guy, but we have nothing in common."

Glory pulled off her robe and turned out the lamp over her bed. "You have nothing in common with a baseball player from Cuba. Forget him," she said as she climbed into bed. "Good night, Rosie."

"Um, Glory, that's another thing," I said. "Rosie was a great name for me when I was little, with floppy ponytails, but I've grown up. Would you mind calling me Rose?"

As Glory rolled over in bed, pulling the blanket up to her chin, she snorted.

"What's that all about?" I asked.

The blanket muffled what she said, but the words were clear enough. "Does this name change involve a blue diamond necklace?"

"You know it doesn't."

"Or an iceberg? I saw the movie too."

"You're not funny," I said.

Glory gave a light snore, pretending to be asleep.

A few minutes later, I climbed into bed and turned out the light. I lay in the darkness thinking about Ricky, surprised that I was still shaken by his kisses.

As Becca had reminded me, in *Titanic* Rose Calvert had been only seventeen when she met

Jack, the one true love of her life. I wouldn't be seventeen for another two months. Was I old enough to fall in love for real?

I had no idea. All I knew was that I had never been kissed the way Ricky had kissed me.

I shivered and tingled as if I were cold, but at the same time I felt warm all over. Had I met my own one true love?

If I had, then what in the world was I going to do about it?

I was beginning to doze off into a warm, cozy dreamworld when a question popped into my mind with such urgency my eyes flew wide open. The security chief and his men had come directly to deck twelve to arrest Ricky. They'd been tipped off about where to find him. But by whom?

AT SEVEN A.M. THE SHIP, GILDED BY THE EARLY-MORNING sunlight, docked at the port of Ocho Rios, Jamaica. I leaned on our balcony railing and looked down at the long, wide, wooden pier, where seamen were busy securing a gangway leading to the boarding area on deck one. Beyond the pier was a port-of-entry building and a parking lot, where tour buses and taxis were already crowded into every available space.

On the other side of this official area I could see a paved road that apparently led up a hill into town. A crowd of people edged the road, with a steady stream of others joining them. Some carried what looked like homemade cardboard signs. Others unfolded bundles. Merchandise for sale? At this distance I couldn't make it out.

As Glory walked out onto the balcony, I asked, "What are all those people doing?"

"Waiting for the tourists who will walk into town," Glory answered. "Many of them have brought souvenirs to sell. The main industry on this island is tourism." She looked at her watch. "Are you ready for a quick breakfast? Our bus leaves for the falls at nine."

"Glory," I said hesitantly, "Ricky is going to be awfully lonely shut up in his stateroom all day. I can stay on board and keep him company."

Glory fixed me with a steely gaze. "That is not an option," she said.

"Then could I just say hello to him before we go to breakfast?"

"A quick hello. That's all."

Glory stepped aside as we left our stateroom, waiting while I crossed the passageway and raised a hand to knock on the Urbinos' door.

"I'm sorry, miss," the guard said. He leaned from his chair and stretched out a hand to stop me. "The prisoner is not allowed to communicate with anyone while we are in port."

I stared in surprise. "I wasn't planning to go inside the stateroom. I just need to know that Ricky is all right."

The guard leaned back in his chair, stretching, before he answered. "He's fine. He and his uncle had a big breakfast. Room service brought it an hour ago."

Glory stepped forward, taking charge. "Thank you," she said to the guard, and she took my hand as though I were a little kid, leading me toward the stairs.

"We're going to stop off on deck five before breakfast so I can leave my watch and rings in the ship's safe," she said. "I don't want to take any chance on losing them while I'm climbing the falls."

"Glory! You can't climb the falls," I argued. "I've seen pictures of them. The rocks are big and slippery."

"Climbing the falls is part of the tour."

"But they're just for young . . . um . . . well, people my age, not for . . . um . . . grandmothers."

"You think I'm too old to climb the rocks? Just watch me," Glory said. She left me near the end of the counter and walked to the security desk.

Nearby, at the door to the chief purser's office I heard someone say, "There's no sign of him, sir."

Startled—was he talking about Ricky?—I turned to see one of the uniformed crew speaking to the purser.

"Did you check his assigned cabin?" the purser asked.

"Yes, sir." The seaman gave a lower deck number. "And I asked the men who share the cabins next to his. No one heard him leave this morning, and his few things are still there." He paused and added, "I even checked with the guard assigned to stateroom

seventy-two-seventy-nine. He said no one had tried
to make contact with Mr. Urbino except the girl in
the stateroom across the passageway."

My face grew hot with embarrassment, but at
the same time I felt a welcome rush of relief. It
wasn't Ricky they'd been talking about. I listened
even more intently.

"The captain ordered him to leave the ship as
soon as possible after we docked," the purser said.
"Did you check the departure area on deck one?"

"I've been in phone contact. He hasn't been
seen there."

They had to be talking about Major Cepeda, I
decided. On a ship this large I could see why someone might be hard to find. If the major had left his
belongings in his cabin, he was probably in one of
the dining rooms or cafés eating breakfast. Had they
thought of checking there? I hoped they'd find him
soon. I didn't trust him. I'd be glad when Major
Carlos Cepeda left the ship.

Glory appeared, smiling broadly. "This is going
to be a great day," she said. "The weather's perfect,
Rosie. Come on. I'm starved for something magnifi-
cent and full of calories, like a cheese omelette and
hash browns. Let's eat!"

———

An hour later, Glory and I crossed the asphalt
parking lot, heading for our tour bus. I glanced to
each side of the lot, looking for Neil, but there was

no sign of him. Glory had said he'd be with our excursion group. So where was he?

Not watching where I was going, I had to jump aside as someone hurried past. "Hey!" I started to say, but stopped in surprise as I saw it was Mr. Urbino.

He didn't speak, and I was sure he hadn't even seen me. He seemed too intent on where he was going. As I followed Glory to the tour bus, I kept watching Mr. Urbino. Dressed in a casual gray shirt, slacks, and jacket, he passed the rows of buses, going directly to a taxi dispatcher. It took only a moment before he was in a cab and the driver was swinging in a wide turn to head up the road into town.

To my surprise, I saw that I wasn't the only one who had been watching Mr. Urbino. Stepping from the shade under the overhang of the port building, Anthony Bailey looked after the cab for a second, then turned and walked back into the building.

That's strange, I thought. It seemed almost as though Mr. Bailey had expected Mr. Urbino to come this way and had been watching for him.

"Here's our bus," Glory said. "Give me a hand on that first step. It's a high one."

"I'll be right back, Glory," I said quickly. "I have to ask someone a question."

Without waiting for an answer, I ran to the taxi dispatcher, who saw me coming and waved to the next cab in line.

"No thanks. I'm not taking a cab," I said. "I want to ask you about that man who just got into a taxi a moment ago—where was he going?"

The dispatcher looked surprised. "Airport," he said. "You want taxi to airport?"

"No thanks," I said again. I backed away, suddenly embarrassed by having given in to my curiosity. "I—I'm traveling by ship."

And so are you, Mr. Urbino, I thought. *What business do you have at the airport?* I ran back to join Glory, who was waiting for me next to the bus.

"What was all that about?" she asked.

"Mr. Urbino took a cab to the airport," I answered. "I don't know why."

"My, aren't you nosy? Maybe he was going to meet a friend. Or pick up a package. Does he need to give you a reason?"

Even more embarrassed, I shook my head. "I know. It isn't any of my business what Mr. Urbino does."

"Or other Cuban baseball players," Glory said. She held out a hand so I could give her a boost up the first step onto the bus.

I didn't agree that Ricky's welfare wasn't any of my business. I believed in his freedom, and I was standing up for what I believed in. Wasn't that what Mom and Glory wanted of me?

As I followed her onto the bus, I tried to keep my mind on the day's trip ahead. Ricky might not like being cooped up, but he would be safe. The captain was tough. The chief of security was tough. And I'd see Ricky that night, after we set sail.

Along with most of the members of our tour group, Neil and Julieta had already gotten on the bus by the time Glory and I climbed aboard. Julieta, perched in the window side of a double seat, snuggled closer to Neil and wiggled her fingers at me.

Neil, who was again covered by a brightly colored long-sleeved shirt and his straw hat with the wide, drooping brim, immediately slid across the cracked brown vinyl and jumped to his feet. Although there were plenty of available seats on the bus, including the two across the aisle, Neil graciously offered his seat to Glory.

Beaming at him, she accepted, but before she could sit down, Julieta scooted from the seat and plopped into the one across the aisle. "I'll sit with Rosie," she said.

Tucked in by the window, I glanced around Julieta, who was animatedly talking across the aisle to Neil. I wanted to giggle at the look on my grandmother's face. *Julieta one, Glory zero*, I thought.

In a way I was glad that Julieta had been so skillful in deciding where each of us would sit. The bus carried us a short distance, past flowering shrubs and ferns interspersed with tall mahogany-and-blue trees our driver called mahoes. I took a few photographs through the windows. But soon my thoughts returned to the short, quiet time

Ricky and I had had on the darkened deck the evening before.

The skin on my upper arms prickled, as if it still felt the grip of Ricky's fingers, and for an instant it was hard to breathe. I had never felt this way about a boy. For the first time I understood how Rose Calvert could believe with all her heart that Jack Dawson was her true love. Rose Calvert and Jack. Would it be Rose Marstead and Ricky?

But Rose and Jack's love had ended in a terrible tragedy. I shivered.

Julieta swiveled to look at me, raising one eyebrow. "You okay?" she asked.

I nodded. "I guess someone must have walked across my grave."

"Your grave? Weird," Julieta said.

"That's an old expression people use when someone shivers," I tried to explain, but Julieta had already turned her attention back to Neil.

The bus parked close to the rush of water that ran from the falls into the sea. Edged by thick, lush greenery, the river splashed and foamed over smoothed limestone rocks dotted with tourists. Clinging, grunting, squealing, they gripped each other in human chains led by guides who scrambled upward.

I turned away from the window. "Are you sure you want to do this?" I asked Glory.

Glory made a face but began to take off her

shoes. "How can I possibly say I visited Dunn's River Falls but didn't climb them?" she answered.

"Stubborn," I mumbled.

But Glory smiled and said, "Stubbornness runs in the family."

I hurried to remove the T-shirt and shorts I'd put on over my bathing suit and followed Glory off the bus to join our own chain of climbers.

Here and there on the six-hundred-foot climb the going was difficult. Once a powerful gush of water undercut my footing on the slippery rocks, knocking me off balance, but Neil tugged me to my feet with such ease I was surprised at his strength. I had to admit I was having a good time.

Later, Glory somehow maneuvered to sit with Julieta both at the café where our group had lunch and on the bus during the rest of the sightseeing tour. I smiled as I thought, *Julieta one, Glory two.*

On the last part of the tour, as the bus headed back to Ocho Rios, Neil leaned across me to point to the top of a vine that had spread across a wall like splashed paint, its scarlet blossoms glowing in the deep afternoon sunlight. "Look!" he said with awe in his voice. "Hovering over the vine. There's a *Papilio homerus*, the large swallowtail butterfly. They're found nowhere in the world but Jamaica."

"Oh," I answered absentmindedly. We'd soon be back at the dock. Ricky had been confined alone in his stateroom all day . . . unless his uncle's trip to the airport had been a short one. It wasn't fair to treat Ricky as a prisoner.

"Their wingspan can grow to a width of thirty feet, and they're often used to carry heavy packages."

"Um," I said. But Ricky could have the run of the ship after it sailed at six that evening. That was what the captain had promised. Surely he'd keep his promise.

"They're easily trainable and can quickly pick up a vocabulary of forty to fifty words—in French, of course."

I blinked and sat up straight as I suddenly realized what Neil had just said. "Wh-what?" I stammered.

"Don't worry about Ricky," Neil said. "He's perfectly safe on the ship."

I felt myself blushing again. Was I that obvious? "I'm sorry I wasn't listening," I said, fumbling for the right words to say. "I was thinking about what a good time we all had today while Ricky was stuck in his stateroom. I guess I felt a little guilty."

Neil smiled, relaxing against the back of the seat. "That was it? I thought maybe you were wishing he was here with you instead of me."

My face grew even warmer. "Don't try to be a mind reader, Neil. You're not very good at it. Tell me more about the so-called giant butterflies instead."

"They really are giants among butterflies," Neil said. "Fourteen-centimeter wingspan. Can you believe it?"

"If you say so," I answered. Instead of trying to convert centimeters to inches, I said, "Ricky will be under guard again while we're in Cozumel, and he's sure to be watched when we reach Miami. How is he going to get away from his guards and onto United States soil?"

Neil thought a moment. "I don't know," he said. "But if you can come up with a plan, count on me to help."

"Thanks," I said. Once again I realized that Neil was really a very nice guy.

The tour bus's last stop before we reached the ship was at a small shopping area on a narrow, tourist-clogged street cluttered on both sides with small souvenir, cigar, and jewelry stores. While a few of the people on the bus headed for shops selling duty-free gold and diamond jewelry, most entered the souvenir shops, returning laden with seed necklaces, straw hats, small wood carvings, and bags of Blue Mountain coffee.

It took little more than five minutes for our bus to return to the parking lot near the dock. Tired and sticky from the humidity, I trudged after Glory across the hot asphalt, with Neil at my side and Julieta bringing up the rear.

A fishing boat, pungent with the smell of fish, was tied to the side of the dock near us. Clustered on the dock above the boat, staring down into the hold, were a number of bystanders.

"Must have a big catch," Glory said. "What would they fish for here? Snapper?"

"Could be shark or barracuda, to draw that much interest," Neil answered.

"Let's go and see," Julieta said. She snatched at Neil's hand and took a step forward.

"Why? It's hot, and I'm sticky. Besides, I'm not that interested in fish," he told her.

"If it's a big shark, I want to see it," Julieta said. She hurried ahead, tugging Neil after her.

I walked behind them, squeezing into an empty space at the side of the dock next to Glory, and stared down into the open hold of the boat.

There, bent over a tangled web of netting, stood two uniformed men who were probably local police, one man in a business suit, and two officers from the ship. One of the ship's officers, who had been down on one knee, got to his feet, and the others moved back.

"Did you get the piece of fabric that was twisted in his right hand?" the ship's officer asked one of the uniformed men.

"Yes." The man held up a scrap of light blue cloth, then dropped it into an envelope. "It looks like a pocket from a shirt."

"Torn off in a struggle?"

"Could be."

"Do you think it could have been robbery?" the

ship's officer asked. "His wallet's in his pocket, but his jewelry is gone. As I remember, on the ship he wore a large gold ring with his initial on it."

The man in the business suit said, "As you see, the bruise is on the left side of the head. Must have been a left-handed assailant."

Someone else spoke but I didn't hear what was said. My attention was riveted on the body lying in the fishing nets. Even with the dark bruise that discolored the left side of his head, it was easy to recognize the Cuban military officer, Major Carlos Cepeda.

I STIFLED A CRY AND TURNED, HURRYING AWAY FROM the edge of the dock. Glory, Neil, and Julieta followed me.

Glory's face was pale, and she clung to my arm. "How awful," she whispered. "I heard them say that man was on the ship with us."

"He's the officer who came aboard to arrest Ricky and take him back to Cuba," I answered. "He's the one who left those flyers offering a reward for Ricky." I gulped, fighting the queasiness that rolled in my stomach. I couldn't erase from my mind the dark, sightless eyes that stared upward. "He's Major Carlos Cepeda."

I wished there were a place to sit down. My legs wobbled, and the air seemed thick and hard to breathe. "When did this happen?" I wondered aloud.

Julieta shrugged. "Probably early this morning. The fishermen found his body about a mile out."

I stared at Julieta. "How do you know?"

"The men were talking. Didn't you hear them?" Julieta shrugged again, as if the question were unimportant, but two pink spots burned in her cheeks.

"No, I didn't hear them," I said.

"Then you should have been listening—like I was."

Glory turned to Julieta with interest. "What else did you hear about his death?" I was thankful to see that color had returned to her face. The frail, shaken woman had disappeared, and she looked more like the strong, in-charge Glory I was used to.

Julieta paused for a moment. "Nothing," she answered. She looked at me and added, "The major should have stayed in Cuba, where he belonged."

"The guy's dead. Don't sound so bitter," Neil told her.

"I'm not bitter," Julieta said. "I just think the major got what he deserved. It's because of Castro's people, like Major Cepeda, that I never saw my grandparents."

It suddenly occurred to me that Julieta hadn't been surprised when I'd told her who Major Cepeda was. "You knew he had come to arrest Ricky," I told her.

Julieta met my stare. "I told you not to keep secrets from me. I find out everything."

Neil sheepishly cleared his throat. "Julieta asked me where Ricky was, and I told her he was under house arrest, so she asked why. It wasn't exactly secret knowledge. With those flyers out offering a reward for his return to Cuba, most of the people on the ship would have known about him sooner or later."

"Neil is right," Glory said. She patted his arm. "We can't do anything here. Let's get back to the ship."

I dutifully walked with the others down the long pier toward the ship. Glory and Neil were talking about the climb up the falls, but I didn't join their conversation. I was aware that Julieta was just as silent. Maybe the sight of Major Cepeda's body had disturbed her, too.

I had been shaken by the photographs of Raúl's body, but the lifeless body of Major Cepeda was even harder to take. There was no way his death could have been an accident. I knew it wouldn't be easy to fall from an upper deck. There were plenty of barriers and railings. Even though I wanted to believe that Major Cepeda had simply fallen, hitting his head on the way down, I knew the police and ship officers were right. It had to be murder. In the darkness, before the faint morning light would draw out the early joggers, someone had probably struck the major, killing him or knocking him

125

unconscious, then dumped him over the railing, sure that his body would never be found.

But who would lure the major to the top deck? And how? From what I'd overheard, it was a left-handed person wearing a light blue shirt. Among nearly three thousand passengers, how could that person be found?

I breathed a sigh of relief as I realized that Ricky had been under guard the entire night. There was no way he could be a suspect.

But what about his uncle, who had left the ship and taken a taxi to the airport? Had he abandoned Ricky? Had he run away?

Was Martín Urbino a murderer?

No! I told myself. *Don't even think like that. Ricky's uncle is going to do everything he can to help him reach freedom, not hurt his cause.*

As I stepped onto the ship's gangway, I hoped with all my heart that Ricky's uncle Martín had already returned.

If the major had been pitched overboard, it was a good guess that the weapon had been too. No weapon. No eyewitnesses. As I followed Glory to our stateroom, I tried to think of what would happen next. A murderer was on this ship, and no one knew who it was.

Glory opened the stateroom door and stepped inside, but I had a question that still needed an answer. I walked over to the guard at Ricky's stateroom door. "Were you on duty here last night?" I asked.

He nodded, so I went on. "Could you testify that neither of the Urbinos left the stateroom during the night?"

He sat up straight and really looked at me for the first time. "Could I testify? What are you talking about?"

"What you know to be true. That neither of them left the stateroom until this morning."

He frowned, studying me. "I still don't see what you're getting at."

I was pretty sure he hadn't heard yet about the major's death. I wasn't going to tell him. I just wanted an answer to my question. "You're guarding the stateroom. You would have kept Ricky Urbino from leaving at any time during the night, wouldn't you?"

"Of course. That's my job."

"What about his uncle?"

"That's not my job. He has the freedom of the ship."

"Was he in the stateroom all night too?"

"Sure." The guard nodded.

"Thanks," I said, smiling with relief.

But he added, "Until about four A.M. He told me he couldn't sleep. He was going to the library to read. He was gone for over an hour."

"Thanks," I said again, although it was hard to

speak. The guard would have no way of knowing whether Mr. Urbino had really visited the library or had gone to the top deck to meet Major Cepeda. No one would know except Mr. Urbino himself. I needed to talk to Ricky.

According to the ship's schedule, that evening's dinner was black-tie, so I showered and then dressed with care in my creamy satin formal. After I had swept up my hair in what my mother called a French roll, I added the pearl earrings and necklace Glory had given me for my sixteenth birthday.

Glory took one look at me and said, "Wow! You look gorgeous! Neil's going to be knocked out."

I sighed and rolled my eyes. "Glory, I'm not interested in impressing Neil."

"Why not? He likes you. I can tell."

"You're imagining things. He's just a nice, polite, friendly guy."

"Just what I told you in the beginning. The right kind of date for you. I'm glad you've come around to my way of thinking."

Frustrated, I tried to explain. "Glory, I haven't come around to your way of thinking, and I don't need anyone to find dates for me. Neil is . . . well, he's just Neil."

"And you're involved in some silly romantic notion about a boy who is soon going back to Cuba," she said, her eyes flashing.

This was not a contest I could win—not without

an argument, and there wasn't going to be one. Glory had been supergenerous to take me on this cruise and to do so many nice things for me. I picked up my small beaded handbag and walked to the door. "You're right about Neil being a nice guy," I said. "Are you ready to go to dinner?"

⸺　⸺

But Neil wasn't just Neil . . . not in a tuxedo. Even though the lapels were a little too wide and the sleeves too short, he still looked terrific. *But then*, I reminded myself, *what guy isn't handsome in a tux!*

He looked surprised as he glanced at me. "You look different all dressed up," he said.

"Should I take that as a compliment?" I asked.

For a moment he looked totally puzzled. Then he said, "Well . . . yeah."

It was kind of funny, in a weird way. Being able to spout baseball scores would have impressed him more than the way I looked in my formal. Not that I had any interest in impressing him.

Across the way I saw Ricky walk into the restaurant alone and sit at the table assigned to him and his uncle. He wasn't wearing a tux, but over his slacks he had on a dark sports coat, white dress shirt, and tie. Even without the glamour of evening wear, he looked wonderful to me.

I glanced from Ricky to the empty chair across our table. "Where's Mrs. Evans?" I asked.

Mrs. Duncastle leaned across Neil to tell me, "Poor Myra is worn out from the shopping tour we went on. She has no stamina—at least not as much as I had at her age."

"She won't be here for dinner?"

"No. She's having room service."

"Rosie," Glory began.

I heard the caution in her voice and knew she was mind reading, so I spoke a little more loudly, hurrying to ask everyone at the table, "Would anyone mind if I invited a friend who's alone to join us for dinner?"

Our waiter arrived, cheerfully greeting everyone as he handed out the evening's menu. All the women smiled and nodded at me and told me they'd be glad to meet my friend. Glory alone was silent, the expression on her face telling me that she wasn't pleased with what I was doing.

Pretending I hadn't received her message, I pushed back my chair and hurried to Ricky's table.

As he looked up at me, his eyes widened, and he smiled. Rising to his feet, he stumbled, catching my hand for balance. "You are a most beautiful Rose," he said. He raised my hand to his lips.

Knowing that everyone at our table was probably watching, I breathed deeply, forced my heart to slow down, and took a step back. "Will your uncle be joining you for dinner?" I asked.

Ricky lowered his voice. "Uncle Martín has left the ship."

"Where is he?"

"Somewhere in the United States by now, I hope."

I clung to Ricky's hand, suddenly frightened. "Why did he leave you? Was it because..." I couldn't finish.

Ricky didn't seem to notice. "He has friends with connections. He is hoping to gather some strong support for me so that I will not be detained and returned to Cuba when I reach the United States."

"Then it wasn't..." Again I stopped in midsentence.

"Wasn't what?" Ricky looked puzzled.

It seemed obvious that he hadn't heard about Major Cepeda, and there was no way I could break the news easily. "Ricky," I blurted out, "Major Cepeda's body was found by some fishermen."

"His *body*?" Ricky sat down suddenly. "What do you mean by that?"

"There was a large bruise on his head. He either fell from the ship, striking his head on the way down, or he was ... he was ..."

"Or he was murdered," Ricky said. "Isn't that what you are trying to say? Rose, my uncle would never be guilty of this."

"I didn't say he was."

He looked up at me. "Don't even think it. Neither Uncle Martín nor I had anything to do with Major Cepeda's death."

"I believe you," I said. And I did. I took him at his word, but there were questions I needed to ask.

"Ricky," I said, "last night you were confined to your stateroom. With a guard at the door there was no way you could have left during the night. But according to the guard, your uncle left the stateroom to read in the library between four and five this morning."

I could see the wheels turning in Ricky's mind. His expression changed from defensiveness to concern. "My uncle *did* leave," he said in a low voice. "He awoke before dawn. He was restless. He had told me his plans to fly to the United States, and he could not sleep. He wanted to read for a while without disturbing me."

Taking a deep breath, I quickly said, "Don't get angry with me for asking. I want to make sure your uncle won't be accused of the crime. Was he wearing a light blue shirt?"

"I don't know what he was wearing," Ricky said.

"Does he have a light blue shirt—maybe a polo shirt with a pocket?"

"Yes."

Feeling even worse about the answers, I came to the last question. "Is your uncle left-handed?"

Ricky smiled. "Neil could answer that for you. Uncle Martín was famous as a left-handed batter."

At the moment all I could think of regarding baseball was "three strikes and you're out."

Ricky watched me intently, his eyes filled with hope. "Were these the right answers?" he asked.

"I don't know," I mumbled. Maybe Mr. Urbino was responsible for Major Cepeda's death, and maybe he wasn't. The only way to find out was to discover who really had committed the murder.

I couldn't do it alone. I needed help from someone who would think logically and not be biased one way or the other. Ricky would definitely be biased. Julieta, with her hatred for the Cuban government, would too. Only Neil could be objective—Neil, who was a reliable, nice guy. Yes. I'd talk to him about it as soon as I could.

Motioning toward our table, I said, "Ricky, this is no time for you to be alone. Please join us for dinner."

"You are right," Ricky said. A faint smile flickered on his lips. "I need to be with someone. I want to be with you."

He stood, and I realized I was still holding his hand. Was I comforting him, or was he comforting me? "Rose," he said, again sliding softly over the sounds in my name, "Uncle Martín will do what he can to help me gain political asylum."

"Will he be able to get you off the ship onto United States soil?"

Ricky shrugged. "He will do his best."

And so will I, I promised myself, although I still had no idea what I—or anyone else—could do.

When we arrived at the table, I introduced Ricky to everyone. All the women were gracious, but no one bothered to hide her curiosity.

"I know we've never met, but you look familiar," Mrs. Applebee said to Ricky.

Glory smiled, but there was no warmth in her smile.

"Who's he?" Mrs. Fleming shouted in Ricky's direction.

"He's a friend, Grandma," Neil said into her ear.

"No, he's not my friend. I've never seen him before in my life," she answered.

Neil pointed to his chest and to me. "*My* friend. *Rose's* friend. His name's Ricky."

Mrs. Fleming nodded and smiled at Ricky, seemingly satisfied.

Ricky and I sat down and gave our orders to the waiter, who immediately brought us all small appetizer plates, on which were toast rounds, chopped egg, a creamy cheese spread, and dollops of shiny black caviar.

Glory unbent enough to lean forward. Her stiff smile still in place, she spoke to Ricky as she would to a small child. "Do you know what this is, Mr. Urbino?" she asked. "Have you ever had caviar? Do you know how to eat it?"

I was so embarrassed I almost groaned aloud.

Ricky chuckled. "I have never eaten caviar, but I shall follow your good example, Mrs. Marstead."

Glory blushed slightly, and Mrs. Duncastle

laughed. "You're one up on us, Ricky, chomping down on caviar at your young age. Out in west Texas we had no idea what caviar was until the seventies, when our husbands all made it big in the oil business."

With the tip of the small knife on her plate Glory added some caviar and chopped egg to a toast round. "Why don't you tell us what life is like in Cuba, Mr. Urbino?" she asked.

"You come from Cuba?" Mrs. Betts asked.

"Yes," Glory answered before Ricky could. "I believe you saw his photograph on that flyer we passed around yesterday."

Mrs. Applebee gave a little shriek. "The photo? The murderer! That's why you look familiar!"

"Ricky is *not* a murderer," I told Mrs. Applebee. "Those flyers were an attempt to frame him for a crime he didn't commit. The captain is satisfied that Ricky is innocent."

Anthony Bailey, smooth in a designer tuxedo, suddenly loomed over my chair. I jumped at the unexpected bellow of his voice behind me. "No matter if he committed a murder or not, the reward is for the young man's return to Cuba," Mr. Bailey said. "Someone might be interested in collecting that reward." I twisted and looked up at him. Mr. Bailey certainly had no need for the reward money, yet he was staring intently at Ricky.

"Who?" I asked. "Ten thousand dollars is not such a big reward."

"Ten thousand dollars plus the perk of getting onto the Cuban government's good side," Mr. Bailey said, and chuckled. "That could make the value shoot over the top."

I gripped the arms of my chair tightly and tried to stay calm. "The captain is going to turn Ricky over to the INS when we get to Miami," I said. "Ricky's going to ask the United States for asylum."

"That won't work," Mr. Bailey said to Ricky, "no matter how much influence you think you've got going for you. They call it wet foot–dry foot."

"What are you talking about?" Mrs. Betts asked him.

"Our government's rule of thumb. If Cuban refugees are caught on land, they can ask for asylum. If they're caught at sea, they have to go back."

For the first time Neil spoke up. "This ship we're on is hardly a makeshift refugee boat, so there are no wet feet here. It's registered in Norway, and the captain is the absolute authority while we're at sea."

Mr. Bailey continued to look directly at Ricky. "It could be worth your while to go back to Cuba."

"To collect the reward for myself?" Ricky said, and I could hear a touch of bitterness in his voice. "It would be hard to spend in prison."

"Not all those who return are sent to prison," Mr. Bailey told him. "Deals can be worked out.

Favors can be called in. Mark what I say: In the future, when all embargoes have been lifted, Cuba's going to be a top tourist center for travelers from the United States. Flashy casinos and great beaches. It's a winning combination. A job with a casino could pay well."

Ricky eyed Mr. Bailey without wavering. "Not for a baseball player," he said. "Especially one in my position. Major Cepeda made that very clear."

Mr. Bailey's voice grew even more gruff. "Major Cepeda did not have good sense. And he certainly had no vision. It is just as well that now he has no say in the matter."

What did Mr. Bailey mean by that? I sucked in my breath, picturing him when he'd first come to our table to be introduced. He had been wearing a light blue shirt.

"Major Cepeda accused me of a murder I did not commit," Ricky said.

This time Mr. Bailey dropped his chin to study me. "I heard why," he said. "I'm sure the Cuban authorities would see the illogic in the frame-up the major invented—just as this young lady did. Think about it."

Then, as though we'd been chatting about the weather, Mr. Bailey smiled, wished us all a happy evening, and left.

Mrs. Applebee continued to stare at Ricky with a scared fascination. "Who was the man they said you murdered?" she whispered.

"Now, Winnie," Mrs. Duncastle began, but Glory interrupted.

"Yes, do tell us," she said. "I believe, from what Rose said earlier, that the murder victim helped you escape from Cuba."

"Glory," I said as our appetizer plates were whisked away and replaced with salads, "please, let's just eat."

Ricky surprised me. "I will be happy to tell the story," he said, and went through the entire sequence of events from the time he left Havana until he joined the ship at Bonita Beach.

The waiter took our empty salad plates, except for Ricky's, which was untouched.

"You haven't told us yet about the murder," Glory said.

Neil broke in. "Let Rose tell us that part," he said. "She's the one who first realized the murder couldn't have happened the way Major Cepeda said it had."

I didn't give Glory a chance to object. I threw Neil a look of gratitude, and while Ricky gulped down his salad, I told everyone what had gone on in the captain's office.

All the women at the table made little sounds of sympathy. Mrs. Betts patted Ricky's hand, and Mrs. Duncastle said, "I'd like to meet your uncle, Ricky. I remember his glory days with the Cincinnati Reds."

The waiter brought our filet mignon, and I began to relax. I cut a small slice of the steak and had it halfway to my mouth when Glory suddenly asked, "Mr. Urbino, something puzzles me. You said you had taken refuge in Neil's stateroom, but the ship's chief of security did not arrest you there. Where were you when you were apprehended? And how did Rosie happen to be with you?"

Ricky didn't hesitate. He looked right into Glory's eyes and said, "Perhaps I was foolish to leave the Flemings' suite. Neil had been very generous to offer me shelter there. But the ship had sailed. I was sure the authorities searching for me had left. I telephoned Rose, who had proved to be a good friend, and asked her to meet me on the open deck."

He stopped and smiled, as if what he had said completely answered her question. Knowing Glory, I was sure there'd be more, so I held my breath, waiting.

"On the open deck," she said.

"Yes. On the deck," Ricky repeated.

"Please pass the salt," Mrs. Norwich said.

"Now, Betty, you know you're supposed to cut down on salt," Mrs. Applebee told her.

"Medical science still hasn't agreed—"

Glory concentrated on her steak, not looking up. I didn't like waiting for what might come next. All I wanted was for dinner to be over.

AFTER A PARADE OF WAITERS CARRYING TRAYS OF BAKED
Alaska, Glory finally spoke to me. "Rosie," she
said, "I'm going to take Eloise to the talent show
and give you and Neil the chance to visit Star
Struck. I understand they've got a band and dancing tonight."

Glory made it sound as if she'd overheard a
random conversation in the passageway, but I
was sure she'd found the information by calling
the desk. I couldn't argue with her—not after
she'd given me this expensive trip. I suddenly
wondered if the way I felt at that moment was
the same way Mom felt every time she did what
Glory wanted.

"Thanks, Glory," I said politely. "Julieta has

been trying to get us to Star Struck ever since we first met on the ship." I turned to Ricky and smiled. "We'll all go."

We said our goodbyes and watched Glory and her friends enter the elevator going down. Instead of waiting for one going up to Star Struck, I pulled Ricky and Neil into the next elevator going down. We got off on seven and went straight to Glory's stateroom.

"We have to talk about Major Cepeda's murder," I told them.

I sat on the bed and waited for Ricky and Neil to make themselves comfortable on the small sofa. Then I repeated to Neil everything Ricky had told me, while Ricky listened. Neil looked stunned.

"Martín Urbino is left-handed," he said.

"I know. That's the problem."

"No, it isn't," he said. "Not if the killer is right-handed."

"The officers in the fishing boat said the wound was on the left side of the head, which probably meant that the killer was left-handed."

"*If* he struck him from the back. I don't think he did."

I stared at Neil for a moment. Suddenly the same idea hit me. "The pocket," I said.

Impatiently, Ricky sat forward. "What are you talking about?"

"A piece of light blue fabric was twisted in the fingers of the major's right hand. The officers who were at the pier said it looked like part of a shirt pocket," I explained. "That means the major may have struggled with someone. They'd be face to face. If that was true, then if the murderer struck out with something, and he was right-handed, he'd hit the left side of the major's head."

Ricky looked at me accusingly. "So we are *not* looking for a left-handed murderer."

"I'm sorry. I had to ask you those questions," I told him. "And we're working it out, just as I told you we would."

Ricky stood and walked to the door. "Come with me, *por favor*," he said.

"Where?" I asked.

"To my uncle's stateroom. We will find the blue shirt. You will see that its pocket hasn't been torn."

"Ricky, I believe you," I said.

"Come," he repeated.

"Let's go," Neil said. He held out a hand and tugged me to my feet. "He wants to convince himself as well as us."

Nervously, I glanced from left to right, but no one was in the passage as we crossed it and entered the Urbinos' stateroom. The room was a twin of ours, even to the muted colors and the prints of ships at sea, but because it was an inside room, it lacked the ocean view and outside light and air.

Ricky pulled a light blue polo shirt from one of the drawers. He unfolded it carefully and held it up. I could see the surge of relief on his face. I felt the same way. "This is my uncle's shirt," he said. "As you can see, the pocket has not been torn."

It was a designer shirt, with an initialed logo in a tiny white crest embroidered on the pocket. But I couldn't help noticing that the label inside the neck had a thick black ink slash across it. I wondered why.

Ricky saw where I was staring. "Neiman Marcus's final sale," he said. "My uncle likes to shop their sales. Sometimes he has sent clothing to Tía Ana and to me. But the salespeople draw a big slash across the labels with permanent ink so what is bought can't be returned. Do you think I should tell the authorities that when they ask to see the shirt?"

"You don't need to tell anyone anything—at least not yet," Neil said. "Fold the shirt again and put it back in the drawer. If the ship's officers ask you about it, you can show it to them. Otherwise, just keep quiet."

"What should we do?" I asked.

"Find out who committed the murder by taking it one step at a time," Neil said.

I sighed. It sounded like an impossible task. "How are we going to do that?"

Neil shrugged. "We could look for the torn shirt. It may still be in the murderer's possession."

Ricky shook his head. "If he tried to get rid of the shirt, it's in one of the trash bins, which will be carted off for disposal when the ship docks in Cozumel."

The idea that we could solve Major Cepeda's murder seemed more and more impossible. "I'm not going to give up," I blurted out. "None of us will. We'll keep thinking about it. One of us is bound to get an idea."

─ ⸺ ⸺

We looked for Julieta at the entrance of the dining room, where people were arriving for the late seating. Julieta was so glad to see us she skipped dinner with her parents so she could go to the club with us. "They've always got stuff to eat up at Star Struck," she said. Looking like a magazine cover model in a clinging pink formal, she took Ricky's left arm and Neil's right, leaving me to trail behind.

The cruise director, Tommy Jansen, looked at me as I entered the room. "Hi," he said. "Want to be useful? Take these and hand them out." He shoved a stack of printed yellow sheets at me.

I shivered as his hand accidentally brushed mine. I remembered what he'd said about getting Major Cepeda out of the way, and I also remembered that the first time I'd seen Mr. Jansen he had been wearing a light blue polo shirt. Was he the murderer?

He glanced at the others but did a double take when he saw Ricky. His mouth opened and shut a couple of times, but he didn't say anything.

Julieta didn't even notice. She began telling Ricky and Neil about the karaoke contest the night before. I wasn't interested, so I idly looked down at the yellow sheets. They were copies of a list that had been handwritten in a round, easy-to-read script and labeled "Scavenger Hunt." Underneath the title was a list of odds and ends. At the top of each page was the next day's date.

Something in my mind suddenly clicked, and I stared with fascination at the list. What a good excuse to go poking around the ship. What a positively *great* excuse!

I scanned the list again and smiled. There was something I could add—at least to the lists the four of us would have.

Against the left wall was a table. From my evening bag I took a small pen and added an item to the list on the top four pages, copying the handwriting.

When I finished, Julieta was still hanging on Neil and Ricky and talking to them and to Mr. Jansen. I interrupted by handing her a copy of the list.

"What's this?" she asked.

"We're having a scavenger hunt all day long to-morrow," Mr. Jansen said enthusiastically. "Lots of fun. Great prizes. Be sure to sign up."

"What are we supposed to find?" Neil asked.

"Here," I said, handing him one of the sheets. "Have a list." I gave one to Ricky, and then I took one and shoved the stack back at Mr. Jansen. He took it and turned to two girls who had just stepped through the open door to the club. He handed the stack to them.

"This is great," I said. "A scavenger hunt is exactly what we need."

"Don't knock it. It can be fun—with the right partner. It's always done in teams of two." Julieta glanced from under her lashes at Neil, then at Ricky, and beamed her smile in both directions.

"I'm not knocking it," I answered, wishing the guys weren't being quite so responsive to her. "I mean it. A scavenger hunt will be perfect. We can go all over the ship and have a good reason for do-ing it."

None of them seemed to get it yet, so I waved my list at them. "Like searching for a photo of a blue shirt," I said, pointing to the item I'd written in at the top of the list.

"A photo of a blue shirt?" Julieta asked. "That's on the list?"

Neil and Ricky stared at me. I could see that they'd finally both figured out what I was talk-ing about.

"I have a camera and you have a blue shirt, don't you?" I asked Julieta.

She made a face. "Oh, that old thing? Not anymore I don't."

"I saw you wearing it on Sunday."

"That was Sunday. It was old and it tore, so I tossed it."

"When?"

"What difference does it make?"

There was no point in making an issue about it. I just shrugged and said, "Never mind."

Neil walked over to where Mr. Jansen stood in the doorway. "Where do we sign up for the scavenger hunt?" he asked.

Mr. Jansen held out a clipboard with a pencil attached. "Right here. Two to a team."

Neil scribbled something, and handed the board to Ricky, who picked up the pencil to write, then looked at Neil. "You and Rose?" he said, startled. "But I wanted—" He turned the pencil to the eraser end, rubbed it on the sheet of paper, then smiled at Julieta and me. "It would be unfair of us not to let you ladies choose your partners for the hunt. You first, Rose. Who do you want to be your partner?"

He knows I'll want to choose him, I thought. My heart gave an extra thump because he was so right. But the scavenger hunt was not a time for romance, and the way I felt about Ricky, I knew I would easily be distracted.

But what if Ricky were paired with Julieta? Maybe the little green jealousy monster got in my way, but I was positive that combination wouldn't help our cause one bit.

As I looked at Julieta, I kept thinking of her hatred for Major Cepeda—a man she'd never even met—and the blue shirt she'd worn and discarded. I needed to find out more about her.

"I choose Julieta," I said.

The three of them stared at me, dumbfounded.

Julieta was the first to speak. "It works out so much better if it's boy-girl," she carefully explained.

"Maybe, if nobody cares who wins, but I'm playing for keeps," I said.

"Rose," Ricky began, but I cut him off.

"We'll start in the morning," I told him. "Then we can get together for lunch, see what we've found, and maybe change partners. Trust me."

He gave me a long, searching look. Then he nodded and turned to Neil. "I guess you and I will be partners," he said.

Julieta's mouth opened in astonishment. "You're going along with this?" she asked. She turned to Neil and asked complainingly, "Neil? Don't you want to be my partner?"

Neil looked uncomfortable. "Sure, but Ricky asked first," he said. He scribbled all our names on the sign-up sheet and handed the clipboard to Mr. Jansen.

More kids began arriving at the club, pushing past us to enter the main room. The four band members began setting up, the lights in the room were lowered to a soft glow, and soon music bounced off the walls.

I folded my scavenger hunt list, tucked it inside my bag, and joined in the fun.

Julieta wasn't just a good dancer. She was a great dancer. And Neil surprised me. He actually had some pretty good moves.

"I watch MTV," he explained.

Ricky had his own way of dancing, but he was terrific during the slow numbers. In spite of the fourteen- and fifteen-year-olds on the floor, who tackled every number with wild energy, every now and then the band played a slow, melt-together kind of tune.

I could have danced with Ricky forever, but time wasn't on my side. The next day we'd be at sea, and the morning after that we'd dock at Cozumel. Saturday we'd be at sea again, and finally, on Sunday morning at eight-thirty, we'd return to Miami. The cruise would come to an end. What would happen to Ricky then? If he was sent back to Cuba or if he remained in the United States, playing for a team in a state far from Texas, would we ever see each other again?

Don't think about it now, I warned myself. *And don't worry about the scavenger hunt tomorrow and what it might bring. Just enjoy this moment.* Taking my own good advice, I lost myself in the music and in the warmth of Ricky's arms around me.

———

Glory woke up when I returned to our stateroom around one in the morning. She turned on a light, struggled to sit up in bed, and asked, "Was he a good dancer?"

"Fantastic," I said. I suddenly realized she was asking about Neil, not Ricky, so I quickly added, "He told me he learned by watching MTV."

Glory chuckled. "Did the others have a good time?"

"Ricky and Julieta? They must have. The band was good. The food was good. Star Struck is a great place."

Looking pleased with herself, Glory slid back down in bed, pulling the covers up to her chin and closing her eyes. "Whenever you think Neil would like to go back to Star Struck with you, just give me the word, and I'll take care of Eloise."

"Thanks, Glory," I said. "Tomorrow there's an all-day scavenger hunt, and we signed up for it."

She opened one eye. "You and Neil?"

"All four of us."

She opened both eyes and drilled me with one of her no-nonsense looks. "Who will be your partner?"

"Julieta," I answered, trying not to smile at the surprised look on Glory's face. "Girls against guys. You know how it is. Julieta and I are going to beat them."

"That's not the way scavenger hunts were done when *I* was young," she mumbled.

I kissed her forehead and teased, "Covered wagons to jets. Times change. You and Eloise will be playing bridge all day. Right?"

"Right." Glory looked smug. "And Dora and I have a good chance of winning." She rolled over in bed, a smile still on her face. "I like to win," she said.

I sat on the edge of the bed and silently took off my shoes. *That's the trouble*, I thought, *but where I'm concerned, it's not a matter of winning or losing.*

Glory loved me—really, truly loved me. So did Mom.

I let the shoes drop to the carpet and tried to think things through. Mom's love wasn't a cake-and-ice-cream kind of love. It was deep and tough, real and strong. But Mom bought the groceries, Glory the presents. Mom paid for braces and flu shots, Glory for parties. What little kid's head wouldn't be turned?

I glanced in the nearby mirror. I wasn't a little kid anymore. I was sixteen—nearly seventeen, old enough to think for myself and to take a stand for what I believed in, just as Mom had been trying to tell me. The moment we got home, I'd let her know I was beginning to understand.

For a moment all that was happening on the ship was overwhelming. I was eager to be home.

CARRYING MY CAMERA, I MET RICKY, NEIL, AND
Julieta outside Star Struck right after breakfast.
"Let's get started," I said.

Julieta looked longingly at Neil and Ricky.
"Are you sure you want to do it this way, Rosie?"
she asked.

"We'll all meet at the café for lunch," I answered. "Twelve o'clock. Okay?"

"Okay," Neil said.

"Come on, Julieta," I told her. "We're going to
start at deck six."

We were in the elevator before she answered,
"What's on deck six?"

"Your stateroom," I told her.

She glanced at me from the corners of her eyes.

"Oh, yeah. I have a bottle of red nail polish, and some of that other stuff on the list."

"And a blue shirt."

Her head snapped up. "I told you. I tossed it."

"Think about it," I said as we arrived at deck six and stepped out of the elevator. I couldn't help being suspicious.

"I have," she said firmly. "No blue shirt. Get it?"

"Where'd you get rid of it?" I asked.

"I don't know. Wastebasket, probably." Her cheeks grew red as she began to get angry. "What difference does it make?"

"It doesn't matter," I answered quickly, trying to calm her down. I was disappointed, wishing I'd been clever enough to make her produce the torn shirt. But I hadn't, so I waited while she filled a carry-on with a few of the small items on the list. "Let's try deck one," I said.

"Nothing's on deck one," Julieta protested. "Just the crew's cabins, the gangway area, and the cargo hold."

"We need a photograph of a blue shirt," I said. "Since we couldn't get one the easy way, we'll have to keep trying. I know that the cruise director has a blue shirt."

I expected Julieta to ask how we were going to find out the number of the cruise director's cabin, but she wasn't thinking in that direction. She was close to pouting as she locked her stateroom door behind us. "This isn't as much fun as if we were with guys."

"We'll switch partners at lunch," I promised.

As we walked back to the elevator, Julieta said, "Ricky's gorgeous, but all he wants to talk about is baseball. I'll take Neil." She thought a moment, blinked, and complained, "But all Neil talks about is baseball too."

I remembered what Tommy Jansen had said to a coworker at the lifeboat drill about a party in his cabin, 2005. I also remembered what he had said when he looked at the flyer offering a reward for Ricky. To my way of thinking, Mr. Jansen was decidedly a suspect, so I led Julieta down the narrow passage and knocked on Mr. Jansen's door.

It took him a while to answer, but he finally opened the door a crack, running his fingers through his tousled hair and squinting, sleepy-eyed. "What's the problem?" he asked.

"No problem. We're on a scavenger hunt," I said brightly.

"Go away," he mumbled, and held his wrist up so he could see his watch. "I had another half hour to sleep before emceeing the morning quiz show, and you wrecked it."

"I'm sorry," I said, knowing I didn't sound one bit apologetic, "but we need a photo of a blue shirt. Do you have a blue shirt?"

His eyes opened wide as he stared at me. "Wait a minute. A blue shirt's not on the scavenger list," he said.

"A *photo* of a blue shirt," I corrected. "It's on ours." I held up my folded, wrinkled sheet of paper.

I could tell by the wary look in his eyes that he was suddenly wide awake and thinking fast, but he sagged against the door, yawned, and tried to look sleepy. In spite of his Broadway experience, he wasn't a very good actor. "Look, kids," he said, "everybody on the ship has a blue shirt. Go find another one. I can grab twenty minutes' more sleep before my alarm goes off."

He banged the door shut.

"We'll try Mr. Bailey next," I told Julieta.

"Who's he?" Julieta asked.

"A friend of a friend," I answered. *And a suspect*, I thought, but I kept the idea to myself.

Julieta frowned. "Why are we doing this the hard way? Why don't we just take a picture of a blue shirt in the gift shop or look for someone wearing one?"

I didn't answer. I just said, "Mr. Bailey is staying in the royal suite."

Her attitude changed immediately. "Wow! I heard that suite even has a piano in it. Do you think we could get a look around?"

I didn't want to see the suite. I wanted to see the condition of Mr. Bailey's blue shirt. But I had to placate Julieta. Shrugging, I said, "Let's go up to deck ten and find out."

We left the drab beige of deck one the moment we entered the colorful elevator with its piped-in music. It was as if the ship proclaimed it was party time again. Julieta chattered the entire way to the door of the royal suite.

To my surprise, the door stood ajar. Silently, Julieta and I looked at each other. She took a step ahead, peeking into the living room of the suite. "It really does have a piano," she whispered.

Someone inside—a woman—began to hum and Julieta jumped backward, bumping into me.

I rapped loudly on the door, calling out, "Hello! Anybody here?"

A uniformed cabin steward carrying a dust cloth came to the door. She smiled and said, "If you girls are looking for Mr. Bailey, he's not here."

I tried to hide my disappointment and held up the list. "We're on a scavenger hunt," I said. "We wanted to photograph his blue shirt."

"Better try somebody else," she told me. "It should be easy to find someone with a blue shirt."

I began to turn away, but Julieta asked, "Could we take a peek at the suite? Just for a minute?"

The steward said, "I can't let you inside. You can see the living room from the doorway, though. Take a quick look so I can get back to work."

What we could glimpse was a vision in cream

and coral, with a white baby grand piano, an elegant glass-and-chrome dining table, and pale, overstuffed sofas. Sprays of baby orchids entwined with clusters of star lilies decorated the coffee table and entertainment center. Morning sunlight poured through the outer glass wall, gilding the room with light.

"Wow!" Julieta said. She glanced coaxingly at the steward. "Couldn't we just take a tiny peek at the rest of the suite?"

The steward shook her head. "Don't even ask."

A deep voice behind us made both Julieta and me jump. "What is the question here? What do you want?"

I turned, so rattled that I blurted out, "Mr. Bailey, we're on a scavenger hunt. We need a photo of a blue shirt. Could we photograph yours?"

He looked steadily into my eyes, as though he could rip out my thoughts and examine them, and I hoped I hadn't made a terrible mistake. "Sorry. I have only one blue shirt, and I sent it with the valet service to be cleaned," he said.

I didn't like the way he kept staring at me. I was positive he had snatched up all my little pieces of memory and knew what I was thinking.

I decided that the best thing Julieta and I could do was to get away as quickly as possible. "I'm sorry to have bothered you," I said, and began to walk back down the passageway.

"You could have introduced me," Julieta said as she followed, trying to catch up with me. "You could have been a whole lot friendlier. Maybe he would have let us see the rest of the suite. I heard it has a hot tub on the balcony."

I reached the elevator and jabbed at the button. "Where are we going now?" Julieta asked. It wasn't a question. It was a complaint.

"To find Ricky and Neil," I answered, which put her into an entirely different mood. By the time we entered the mall on deck five, she was happy again.

It was easy to find them. They were seated in the first place we looked—the bakery—munching on freshly baked cookies. Julieta slid into a chair and plopped our scavenger bag on the table in front of them. "How much were you able to collect?" she asked.

Both Ricky and Neil had the grace to look embarrassed.

"We, uh, met here to plan our approach," Neil said.

"And?" Julieta asked.

"We didn't leave," Ricky admitted. "We got to talking about baseball and other things."

Julieta just raised one eyebrow and moved closer to Neil. "We'll switch partners now," she said.

Ricky smiled at me, but Neil said, "We were going to switch after lunch. It isn't lunchtime yet."

I sat down too. "Don't you want to know what we found?" I asked.

"What?" Neil and Ricky said together.

"No blue shirt," I answered.

Julieta looked exasperated. "I told you, we can photograph a blue shirt in the gift shop! Give me the camera!"

She snatched it off the table and set off across the mall to the row of shops, disappearing inside one of them.

"Mr. Bailey claims his only blue shirt is at the laundry," I said. "And Tommy Jansen wanted to go back to sleep, so he wouldn't help us."

"Did you find out what Julieta did with her blue shirt?" Neil asked.

"She just keeps saying she tossed it."

"Maybe Bailey tossed his, too."

"I know how we can find out," Neil said. "I'll be back in a minute."

He went to the nearby wall phone and we heard him ask the ship's operator to connect him with the laundry. Someone answered right away, and Neil said, "I'm calling about Mr. Anthony Bailey's order. When will it be delivered to his stateroom?"

After a pause, Neil asked, "Is a blue polo shirt with that order?"

"Okay," he said. "I understand. Thank you."

He came back to the table, sat down, and told us, "Mr. Bailey did send some stuff to be cleaned this morning."

"Like a blue shirt?" I held my breath, eagerly waiting for the answer.

"They couldn't tell me," Neil said. "Back to zero."

I wouldn't give up. I said to Ricky, "Why don't we go down to the lower decks and see if we can find the laundry? Someone there might tell us, or we might even be able to see Mr. Bailey's order if it's ready."

Ricky shrugged. "You saw my uncle's blue shirt. It was in good condition. That should be enough to clear him of any suspicion."

"It may not be enough," I insisted. "We need to find out exactly whose pocket ended up in Major Cepeda's hand."

Julieta ran back to the table. She put down the camera, waved the developed photo at us, and dropped it into the bag. "There!" she announced triumphantly. "The photo *and* the pencil stub we needed. I found it at the counter. We've got more than half the things on the list already. Let's see what else we can find."

"Julieta! There you are! Having fun?" A good-looking woman with curly red hair stepped up to our table. She put an arm around Julieta's shoulders and smiled at all of us.

Because she and Julieta looked so much alike, it was easy to see that the woman must be Mrs. Vargas, Julieta's mother. But it wasn't their strong resemblance that interested me. It was what Mrs. Vargas was wearing: white slacks, white sleeveless T-shirt, and a sheer blue blouse.

I glanced at Julieta and saw that she was watching me closely. Her cheeks were a mottled red.

We all stood up as Julieta introduced us to her mother, who smiled, told us all to have fun, and left to join her husband.

As soon as Mrs. Vargas was out of earshot, Julieta glared at me and muttered, "It wasn't *my* blue shirt. It was Mom's, and she wasn't happy that I borrowed it. Okay? Are you satisfied?"

"I'm sorry," I said. "It's because of that scrap of blue cloth they found in Major Cepeda's hand. It came from a blue shirt. We need to find the torn shirt."

Julieta's eyes grew wide. I expected her to lose her temper again, but instead she laughed until tears came to her eyes. Finally, she was able to ask, "Did you really think I murdered Major Cepeda?"

"You said you hated him."

She nodded. "I hate everything about the Cuban government, but I didn't even meet Major Cepeda, let alone kill him." She looked at Ricky. "Is all this about the INS sending you back to Cuba?"

I answered for him. "We're trying to help both Ricky and his uncle."

"Count me in," Julieta said. She took Neil's hand, but he kept his eyes on me. "At twelve o'clock we'll meet at the diner for lunch. Right?"

"Right," I said. "Ricky and I will be there."

As Julieta and Neil left, I tried to keep my mind on what we were supposed to do—look for a light blue shirt with a torn pocket. But Ricky and I would be alone together. It didn't matter if it wasn't the top deck in the moonlight. Being anywhere with Ricky was all I could ask for.

His hand was strong and warm as it gripped mine. Contentedly I rode in the elevator with him down to deck one.

As we stepped into the passage, Ricky came to a sudden stop and looked both ways. "There should be a stairway down the next deck. I think that's where the laundry would be." He led me to a nearby double door and silently pushed it open. Then he turned and smiled. "Stairs. Here they are."

We paused at the head of the stairs, jumping as the heavy doors clanged shut behind us. No one responded to the noise, and we didn't see anyone, so we carefully began to descend. The low, rumbling, purring beat of the ship's engines vibrated below, and our footsteps echoed on the metal floor.

I looked ahead through the dim light at the cargo hold. Tall stacks of boxes and crates were bound together on pallets and fastened to supports, probably so they wouldn't topple in heavy seas. There were company logos on some of the crates, but I had no idea what might be inside them.

In the movie *Titanic*, Rose and Jack found a car in the hold. As they sat in it, they had talked and kissed. I glanced ahead, but the ship we were on carried nothing so romantic.

There was a brightly lighted area at the far end, so we began to walk down one aisle between the crates. I could feel the throbbing of the engines in my head. It was like hearing bass notes without the melody, like being stuck at a stoplight next to a pickup truck with the drumbeat of its radio music slamming the air.

Ricky stopped, putting an arm around my shoulders. "You put too much hope in finding that torn shirt. I don't think Mr. Bailey would send a torn shirt to the laundry. He would just throw it out and buy a new one."

I sagged against Ricky, discouraged. Of course he was right.

The next thing I knew, we had stepped into a narrow walkway between the stacks of crates. Ricky's arms were around me, and his lips were on mine. I kissed him back as eagerly as I had before. There was no one like Ricky. There never would be. Just as Rose Calvert had been sure about Jack's being her one true love, I was beginning to be sure about Ricky.

Abruptly, the clang of the cargo hold's doors interrupted the steady beat of the motors. Ricky and I stiffened, listening intently yet still holding each other tightly.

"Be very silent," Ricky whispered. "Someone is down here with us."

I could hear the slow, heavy footsteps coming closer. Now and then they paused, as if the person had stopped to look around. After each pause they moved on, coming closer and closer.

It could not be one of the crew who worked

here. A seaman would attend to whatever business he had and be gone. The person who was stalking us was probably as unfamiliar with the hold as we were.

Who was he? And why was he hunting for us? I was so frightened I wanted to scream and run, but I couldn't move.

Putting a finger to his lips, Ricky pulled me through the small walkway and into the next aisle. We both stepped softly, placing our feet carefully. I was terrified that we'd make a noise that would let our stalker know where we were.

We could hear him coming nearer but could see nothing over or around the tall stacks of crates. Dizzy with fear, my heart thumping in my chest, I leaned against Ricky. Whoever was in the hold was between us and the door. Ricky and I were trapped.

RICKY TUGGED ME FORWARD ONE SLOW, SILENT STEP AT a time, and I realized that the person who was after us had gone on. I fought a panicky urge to bolt and run. It was hard to breathe and even harder to think, but I followed Ricky, not daring to turn and look back.

Suddenly Ricky stopped. I raised my head and saw that we had come close to the stairway.

"Now!" Ricky whispered.

Still holding hands, we raced to the stairs, scrambled up, and burst through the heavy metal doors, nearly charging into Mr. Wilson, the ship's chief of security.

"Stop right here," he ordered. "Just what were the two of you doing in the hold?"

"Looking around," I answered. "For the scavenger hunt," I added quickly. I glanced at the doors we had come through and saw one of them open just a crack. I felt that someone was staring at us, but I couldn't see who it was.

Mr. Wilson didn't seem satisfied by my answer. "Why'd you fly out of there in such a rush?"

I had to be honest. "Someone was in there with us."

I saw the door slowly being pulled shut.

"Who was it?" Mr. Wilson asked.

"We don't know," Ricky said.

Mr. Wilson shook his head. "No doubt it was one of the crew, and if he'd discovered you, he would have chased you out of there." He looked at Ricky and added, "When I said you'd have the run of the ship while we were at sea, I expected you to know there'd be limits."

He motioned to us to follow him down a short passage. He stopped in front of a door that had a round window in it the size of a large soup bowl. As he swung back the metal plate that covered the window, I heard the elevator doors open and shut. Whoever had been stalking Ricky and me had slipped out of the area. We'd never discover who it was.

"Take a look through here," Mr. Wilson said.

Ricky did first, and when he stepped back, I looked through the window. I saw a small room with thickly padded walls. The only furniture in the room was a twin bed.

"That's our brig," Mr. Wilson said. "I'd hate to have to confine you in there, Mr. Urbino."

Ricky quickly nodded. "I understand. I'll stay in the public areas."

Mr. Wilson looked at his watch. "Until six o'clock. I want you to report to your stateroom at that time. That's when I'll post a guard."

"Six o'clock?" I protested. "But we won't arrive at Cozumel until tomorrow morning. There's dinner and dancing tonight and—"

He interrupted me with a brisk shake of his head. "I'm not in charge of this young man's social life. I've set a schedule that's expedient, and I expect you to abide by it."

"Yes, sir," Ricky said.

"And no visitors," Mr. Wilson said, his eyes on me. "I don't want to give the guard any extra problems."

I didn't dare to argue. At least I would have Ricky until six o'clock.

I looked at my watch. "It's almost noon," I told him. "Let's go up to the diner and meet Neil and Julieta."

In the elevator Ricky pointed out a smear of what looked like black grease on his left shoulder. "I must have rubbed up against something down there," he said. "Do you mind waiting while I change shirts?"

"Not at all," I said. When we reached our staterooms, I remained in the hall while Ricky went into number 7279. I expected him to be quick, but I was surprised when the door burst open again almost immediately. Ricky's face was pale, and he looked as if he was going to be sick.

"Come," he said. "There's something you must see."

I braced myself for whatever I was going to find, so when I entered the stateroom, I was puzzled when Ricky pointed to an open drawer in the cabinet.

At first, I glimpsed what I thought was his uncle's light blue shirt. "What?" I asked. "We've seen the shirt."

"Not this shirt," he said. "Look closely."

I took two steps forward and looked down into the drawer. I saw a light blue shirt, wadded—not folded—and only ragged, torn stitching where a pocket had once been.

"Someone took Uncle Martín's shirt and left this in its place," he said.

"To make the police think he committed the murder," I whispered.

I backed up on wobbling legs and plopped down on the nearest twin bed. "Ricky," I said, "whoever did this will make sure Mr. Wilson and his men find this shirt. Maybe he's notified Mr. Wilson already. We have to get this out of here."

Ricky snatched up the shirt, but he looked around frantically. "Where can we put it?"

"Give it to me," I told him. As I took the shirt, I

examined it. A polo shirt with a Bloomingdale's label. "Bloomingdale's is a big department store. There's a huge one in New York City," I said.

Quickly I pulled out my key card, crossed the passageway to our stateroom, and opened the door. Once inside with the door shut, I opened the bottom drawer in the chest where I kept my folded T-shirts and shorts. I pulled out a blue-and-white shirt and tucked the torn polo inside it, with the collar neatly showing. Satisfied that it looked like a layered shirt, I refolded it and placed it at the bottom of the stack in the drawer.

I then left the stateroom and shut the door, facing Ricky. "If anyone asks you, you don't know where the shirt is," I said.

He nodded and asked, "But if they ask *you*?"

"They won't. How should I know anything at all about your uncle's clothing?"

Ricky rested his hands on my shoulders. I thought he might kiss me again, but he only shook his head sadly. "Rose," he whispered, "when we are safely inside the United States, you and I—"

He didn't finish the sentence. We were interrupted by Mr. Wilson, with two of his men. "Mr. Urbino," he said, "I am looking for your uncle. Is he in your stateroom?"

Ricky stood tall, with his shoulders held back. I heard him take a long, slow breath. "My uncle is not aboard the ship," he said. "He left yesterday, while we were in Jamaica."

Mr. Wilson tried to hide his surprise. "We were not informed of this," he said.

Ricky didn't answer, so Mr. Wilson went on. "Do you know his whereabouts in Jamaica?"

"He should not be still in Jamaica," Ricky answered. "His intention was to book a flight to the United States. He plans to talk to people who might help influence the immigration officials on my behalf."

Mr. Wilson threw him a quick frown. "He might be better off hiring an attorney on his own behalf. We have been given information that..." He stepped forward and added, "The captain has requested that I search your stateroom."

Ricky stepped aside with a nod. Mr. Wilson took out a key card and opened the door.

"You have a key," I said in surprise.

"I have a master key," he said.

Ideas began to fall into place. Bloomingdale's, New York . . . Tommy was from New York . . . Rita, the steward who liked Tommy Jansen and who worked on deck seven . . . She might open the Urbinos' stateroom door for him. "Do the stewards have master keys too?" I asked.

Mr. Wilson ignored me and said to Ricky, "Mr. Urbino, will you step inside with us, please?" I began to follow, but he gave me a sharp look and ordered, "Please remain in the passageway, Ms. Marstead."

I waited outside the stateroom, but I kept the

door from shutting by leaning against it. I had to see what was going on.

Mr. Wilson directed the opening of all the cabinet drawers, and all the clothing inside them was taken out, examined, then returned.

Every inch of that stateroom was covered—the closet, the bathroom, and the sofa. When there was no place else to search, the beds were taken apart.

Mr. Wilson turned to Ricky in exasperation. "Does your uncle own a light blue polo shirt?"

"Yes," Ricky said.

"Can you tell me where it is?"

"No," Ricky answered truthfully. "I do not even know exactly where my uncle is."

Mr. Wilson glanced around, then said, "I'll send someone to help straighten up the room. Until we get matters sorted out, I'm going to ask you to remain here."

"That's not fair," I complained.

"And no visitors." Mr. Wilson looked from me to one of his men and said, "I'll post you here as guard."

As Mr. Wilson stepped into the passageway, I told him, "I saw Major Cepeda's body. I know about the blue cloth that was in his right hand, and I heard one of the policemen say that it looked like a pocket torn from a shirt. You're acting like that shirt belongs to Mr. Martín Urbino, but it doesn't. What makes you think it does?"

He didn't answer, so I went on, "When you came, you told us you had information, but you didn't say who gave you that information. Who told you the torn shirt was in Mr. Urbino's stateroom?"

"That is not a matter for discussion," he said.

"I think it is," I insisted. "Whoever told you that torn shirt was here was trying to frame Mr. Urbino."

Ricky was so upset his face was red and blotchy. "My uncle is not a murderer," he said.

"Mr. Wilson, please tell us who sent you here," I begged.

He gave me a long stare, then softened. "I understand your concern, Ms. Marstead," he said, "but I'm not at liberty to answer your question."

"It was the murderer," I told him, "trying to make you think Martín Urbino was the murderer, instead of himself."

"Why do you say that?"

"Because he—" I wanted to blurt out everything about the shirts that had been switched, but I couldn't, not without knowing who had taken Martín Urbino's blue shirt. "Because he was lying," I finished. It sounded lame even to me.

Before I could even say goodbye to Ricky, his stateroom door was shut, with the guard standing in front of it, and Mr. Wilson was striding down the passageway.

I could think of only one thing to do. I went

back into Glory's stateroom, took a sheet of stationery and an envelope from the desk drawer, and wrote a description of Mr. Urbino's blue shirt, complete with the tiny logo on the pocket and the black slash of permanent ink across the label in the neck. I even drew a sketch of the shirt. Then I signed the page, folded it, and put it in an envelope. I wrote the captain's name on the envelope, then sealed it. It was time to meet Neil and Julieta, but before I did I took the envelope to deck five and gave it to one of the attendants at the desk.

"Promise that the captain will get this letter right away?" I asked.

She gave me a smile right out of the cruise line's commercial. "Right away," she repeated. "I promise."

A few minutes later I reported what had happened to Neil and Julieta. I told them about the torn shirt that had been substituted for Mr. Urbino's shirt, but I didn't tell them what I had done with it. And I told them why I thought the person behind the substitution was Tommy Jansen.

"Let's keep an eye on him the rest of today and tomorrow," I said. "He talked about getting Ricky off the ship in Mexico and said he was beginning to come up with an idea."

"We won't let him out of our sight," Neil said.

Julieta started to say something, but Glory stepped up, taking my arm.

"I thought I'd find you here," she said. She looked around. "Where's Ricky?"

"In his cabin, with a guard outside," I answered.

Glory looked pleased. "Well, the rest of you have fun," she said. "I've got to get back to our bridge lunch, but I wanted to ask if you'd like me to sign you and Neil up for snorkeling tomorrow. Cozumel is supposed to have some of the best beaches in the Caribbean."

Neil looked to me for an answer, and I fumbled to find one that made sense. I couldn't tell Glory we were going to spend our time tailing the cruise director. "Neil has to take care of his grandmother," I said. It was the first excuse I could think of.

"Eloise will be fine with me. Some of our group have been to Cozumel before, so we thought we'd stay aboard and relax by the pool. For you and Neil this is your first trip to Cozumel, so we want you to really enjoy the island."

Without an idea in my mind, I began, "Uh . . . we might go . . . uh . . ."

"Shopping," Julieta said decisively. "The town of San Miguel on Cozumel has the best shopping on this trip. Rosie needs some Mexican silver bracelets. They're inexpensive but beautiful."

"I should buy something for my mother," Neil said.

Me too, I thought. *Like a peace offering.* I ached to make everything all right between us again.

175

Glory looked surprised, but she quickly countered, "It shouldn't take long to shop. How would you like to see the Mayan ruins?"

I would have loved to see the Mayan ruins and visit the caves at Xel-Ha, but Ricky's future was more important. "No thanks, Glory," I said. "We just want to go into Cozumel and hang out."

Glory made it obvious that she didn't like to be challenged. She gave me a firm look, but she said, "All right then. I'll let you and Neil plan your own day." Then she turned her look on Julieta and said, "Julieta, dear, I'm sure you'll want to spend some time with your parents. I do believe they've hardly seen you."

Wisely, Julieta nodded but didn't answer. She and I were the same age, but she was way ahead of me in keeping her cool.

———

Tailing Tommy Jansen the rest of the day wasn't hard to do. He went from awarding T-shirt prizes to the winners of the scavenger hunt, to emceeing a talent show for kids, to announcing for a mechanical horse race, to emceeing a quiz game for senior citizens. Since Julieta ate dinner at the late seating and Neil and I at the early seating, one of us was free at all times to shadow him.

During my break I paid a visit to the store on the shopping level of the ship and bought one of the sunken treasure pendants for Mom. The peace offering I'd wanted. No, it wasn't only a peace offering. It was a gift to show how much I loved her. It wasn't going to be Mom and me or Glory and me. I loved them both.

When Neil and I met Julieta late in the evening at Star Struck, she reported, "Tommy Jansen asked one of the employees who gives that 'Shopping the Caribbean' program to tell him the name of a good jewelry store in Cozumel."

"I thought he was short of cash," I said.

"You told us he had plans to get Ricky off the ship," Neil said. "How would a jewelry store figure in?"

I was thinking hard. "You don't just *buy* jewelry in jewelry stores," I said. "Sometimes you sell to them." I began to get excited. "What if he owns an expensive watch and thinks he can get enough for it for two plane tickets from Cozumel to Cuba?"

"What time do we dock?" Neil asked.

"Seven A.M.," Julieta groaned.

"The stores won't be open that early," I told them. "Anyway, it takes about an hour before passengers can leave the ship."

Neil frowned. "I'll have to make sure my grandmother has had breakfast and is set for the day."

"Then I'll show up at the disembarking area before they allow passengers to go ashore, and I'll watch for Mr. Jansen," I said.

"I'll be with you," Julieta told me, which surprised me.

"Good," Neil said to Julieta. "If Rosie follows Tommy Jansen, she shouldn't be alone. What are the names of the jewelry stores he was told to go to?"

"Just two stores," she answered, and gave him the names and directions. "They're on the main street in San Miguel, near the plaza."

Neil stood and looked at his watch. "It's getting late. I think I'll turn in," he said.

Julieta and I decided to call it a night too.

As we all left Star Struck, I glanced back at Mr. Jansen, who was leading off another round in the trivia contest. *Wherever you're going tomorrow, we're going too,* I thought.

"Rosie," Julieta said quietly, and I realized she had followed my glance. "We're not going to let anyone take Ricky off this ship."

"Thanks," I said, and smiled, wishing I were as confident as Julieta.

Glory was still awake when I reached our stateroom. "I did a little shopping today," she said. "The duty-free store had a special on French silk scarves, so I bought one for you to give your mother."

Looking proud of herself, she opened a thin box and pulled out a square scarf with a swirling design in red, pink, and yellow. I couldn't keep from wincing. Was that what Glory thought Mom would like? It was much too gaudy, and the colors were all wrong for Mom.

"Thanks, Glory," I said politely, "but I've

already bought Mom a present." I took my package out of my drawer and opened the box to show her the pendant.

I could see the conflicting emotions in her face. "It's beautiful," she finally said. "I bet you love it yourself."

I nodded, and she smiled. "Then why don't you keep it for yourself and give the scarf to your mother?"

I closed the jewelry box and tucked it away in the drawer. "I won't. Because I love my mother very much, and I chose this gift for her myself," I said.

Glory drew back, her hurt feelings showing. "I was only trying to do something nice for you," she said.

I put an arm around her. "And nice for Mom," I told her, "which is good, because I love both of you."

Glory was sharp. She got my message. But she didn't give up easily. "Ever since you were born, I've loved doing special little things for you," she said.

"You have, and I'm grateful for them all," I answered. "And Mom is too."

I shouldn't have added that last remark, because Glory turned away, swept the scarf back into its box, and climbed into her bed.

"Goodnight, Glory. Sleep tight," I said.

I bent to kiss her cheek. Sometime I'd have to tell her that when I was little and heard people singing "Glory, glory, hallelujah" from "The Battle

Hymn of the Republic," I thought they were singing about my wonderful grandmother. Gifts had nothing to do with my love for her.

By the time I climbed into bed, my thoughts were once more on what we would find in Cozumel. I had the awful feeling that something terrible was planned for Ricky the next day, and I had no idea how to stop it.

THE EARLY-MORNING SUN WAS ALREADY HIGH AND HOT as Julieta and I hailed a taxi, following Mr. Jansen into the shopping area of San Miguel. On our left, lush bushes of red, pink, and yellow hibiscus decorated the seawall. On the right were buildings whose shops and contents were every bit as colorful. I realized that business hours had been set by cruise ship schedules. This would probably be a busy day for the merchants of San Miguel; three cruise ships had already arrived in port.

As we reached the plaza, I saw Mr. Bailey enter a shop with large signs in Spanish and English cluttering the window: FAX MACHINES HERE. FOTOCOPIAS 4 CENTS.

Before I had time to wonder what Mr. Bailey

was doing, Julieta leaned forward. "Stop here!" she told the driver. She quickly paid him and we climbed from the cab. Pointing at a large *joyería* with impressive necklaces, bracelets, and rings in the window, Julieta said, "Tommy Jansen just went into that jewelry store."

Stopping at the doorway, we cautiously looked around, careful not to let him see us. We spotted Mr. Jansen talking to a woman behind a counter at the back of the store, so we made our way toward him through a number of busy shoppers and clerks.

As we came close, he reached into his pocket and pulled out a large gold ring. "This should be worth a lot," he told the woman. "In dollars. American dollars."

She held the ring high, turning it around as she studied it, so I was able to get a good look at it.

Shocked, I shouted, "Julieta! That's Major Cepeda's ring!"

Mr. Jansen tightly gripped the counter and whirled toward us. He opened his mouth to speak, but was only able to make a gargling sound.

I stepped forward, facing the woman. "That ring belonged to a man who was murdered on our ship," I told her. "Please call the police and ask them to contact Mr. Wilson, the chief of security."

Julieta had blocked the aisle, but Mr. Jansen didn't try to run. He just sagged, leaning against the counter as if he needed it to hold him upright.

Fear was in the woman's eyes as she held the

ring out to me. "Take it. I want nothing to do with it," she said.

As I reached for it, she shoved it into my hand with such force it hurt.

"Ouch!" I said. I opened my hand and saw the red C-shaped mark the initial had made in my palm. Into my mind came the photograph of the beaten and murdered Raúl with C-shaped bruises on his face. So Cepeda was a murderer murdered in turn. I shuddered.

A firm hand was placed on my shoulder, and a familiar voice asked, "Rose? Are you all right?"

I looked up at Neil and nodded. "I'm glad you're here," I told him.

It took only a moment for uniformed *policía* to arrive. They took Mr. Jansen, Julieta, Neil, and me to a small white stucco building, the *comisaria de policía*, and heard the story of the ring and the murdered Major Cepeda.

We repeated our story several times, to a number of people in and out of police uniform. Mr. Jansen interrupted every so often to claim that he had simply found the ring on the upper deck of the ship when he led the early-morning jogging group and had not killed the major.

Finally, someone in authority in San Miguel decided they wanted nothing to do with the matter because it hadn't taken place under their jurisdiction. Two officers drove us back to the ship and escorted us to the captain's office.

"Everyone, please sit down," the captain ordered in a no-nonsense voice. He thanked the Mexican *policía*, who left when Mr. Wilson and his two assistants arrived.

We had to tell the story again, and once more Mr. Jansen interrupted to claim he knew nothing about the murder.

I hated to admit it, but I began to think he could be innocent. I remembered Major Cepeda fiddling with his ring and how I'd thought it was so loose that he could lose it. If he'd struggled with someone on deck before he went overboard, it was certainly possible that his ring had fallen off and Tommy Jansen—first on the scene at daylight—had found it.

"What are your orders, sir? Do you want me to confine Mr. Jansen to the brig?" Mr. Wilson asked.

"You can't do that!" Mr. Jansen answered. "Tomorrow we'll be at sea all day, and there's the miniature golf tournament, the sixties quiz for the baby boomers, the finale for the Broadway show, and the—"

The door to the captain's office flew open and Anthony Bailey stood in the doorway. Without paying the slightest attention to the rest of us in the room, he walked straight to the captain and held two sheets of paper out to him.

"What's this?" Captain Olson asked.

Mr. Bailey looked smug. "It's a signed release from Mrs. Beatriz Urbino, grandmother and official guardian of the minor child, Enrique Urbino, giving

me the right and power to return her grandson to
Cuba. This permission was faxed to me less than an
hour ago."

I took a deep breath and stood. "Captain
Olson," I said, "before you make any decisions, I
think Ricky's attorney should be present." Frantically, I turned to Julieta. "Glory said she'd be relaxing by the pool. Find her! Tell her what happened!"
I clutched Julieta's arm. "Say I trust her promise to
do anything I ask, and now I'm asking."

"Okay," Julieta said. She slipped out the door
and was gone.

The captain didn't look too happy. He kept rubbing his temples. But he said, "Very well. We will
continue our discussion after Mr. Urbino's attorney
is present."

"That's ridiculous," Mr. Bailey protested. "I
have the papers. I have the official permission to return Enri—"

"Please be silent!" the captain thundered. "As I
told you, we will wait until Mr. Urbino's attorney
arrives. Now, please have a seat."

I was sure the captain welcomed the chance to
think about all that was happening on his ship,
which was supposed to involve his passengers in
nothing more than a pleasure cruise.

As we waited, I took a good look at him, and I
nearly hyperventilated. Mr. Bailey was wearing a
light blue polo shirt with a tiny logo embroidered in
white over the breast pocket.

I whispered to Neil, "Look at the shirt Mr. Bailey's wearing. I think it's Martín Urbino's shirt."

There was a polite knock at the door before Glory and Julieta walked in. Glory, in a gauzy white cover-up over her one-piece black bathing suit and red flip-flops, walked straight toward the captain and held out her hand. "I'm Gloria Marstead, attorney for Enrique Urbino," she told him. "I believe I understand the situation, and I also believe that the proper jurisdiction for any action on the part of Enrique Urbino is with the Immigration and Naturalization Service in the United States."

Glory didn't look much like an attorney, but she sounded like one. The captain looked relieved. "My thoughts exactly," he said.

"Wait a minute," Mr. Bailey protested.

He began to rise from his chair, but the captain scowled and said, "Sit down, Mr. Bailey. We will resolve this problem in an orderly fashion."

Mr. Bailey didn't give in easily. "I have the right to remove the minor, Enrique Urbino, from the ship immediately and take him to Cuba. You saw the papers I gave you."

"May I see them, please?" Glory asked.

Captain Olson handed them to her, and she quickly read through them. She looked up and said, "At first glance, they seem to be in order. However, since they are faxed, there is a question about their authenticity. I suggest that when we land in Miami, these papers be turned over to the INS for evaluation."

"I agree," the captain said.

Mr. Bailey jumped to his feet and grabbed Glory's arm. "Now, you listen here!" he began.

He didn't get a chance to continue. Mr. Wilson, his men, and Neil grabbed him, dragging him away from Glory.

I got into the mix-up, too, because I had to see the label on that blue polo shirt. I snatched for the back of the shirt collar and gave it a twist as Mr. Bailey was dumped back into his chair.

"Sit down!" the captain demanded. "Everyone— sit down!"

I did what he said, but I asked, "Captain Olson, did you get my letter with the description of Martín Urbino's blue polo shirt?"

"Yes," he said. "I gave it to Mr. Wilson."

"Mr. Bailey is wearing that shirt," I said, and I told them about the ink slash on the label. "Mr. Bailey substituted his torn shirt for Mr. Urbino's shirt to make you think Mr. Urbino had killed Major Cepeda. Then he phoned you to tell you where the shirt was—didn't he, Mr. Wilson?"

Mr. Wilson addressed the captain, not me. "Yes," he said, "but when we searched Mr. Urbino's stateroom, we did not find the shirt."

"I know where it is," I said, "but first, will you answer an important question? Was Mr. Bailey the one who let you know where you could find Ricky when you arrested him?"

"Yes."

"Mr. Bailey is the murderer," I said.

"You can't prove anything," Mr. Bailey said.

"You wanted to ingratiate yourself with Castro and the Cuban government officials so you can build your supercasino in Havana," I told him. "That's what you wanted—not the reward money. You approached Major Cepeda, but he wouldn't cooperate with you. Those flyers he handed out were to turn people against Ricky and intimidate him into returning. I would guess there was no reward at all. Major Cepeda wanted the glory of bringing Ricky back, and he wouldn't let you share it. Isn't that right? So you decided to get the major out of your way."

"Prove it," Mr. Bailey growled.

The captain looked from me to Tommy Jansen. "But Mr. Jansen was in possession of the major's ring," he said.

"The ring was loose on the major's finger," I said. "You saw him fiddling with it when we were all here in your office. I believe Mr. Jansen. I think he really did find it on deck while he was jogging."

Mr. Bailey kept glaring at me, and I saw Glory watching him with a frown. She said to the captain, "If you'll accept my suggestion, sir, for safety reasons I'd incarcerate Mr. Bailey until we land in Miami and he can be turned over to the proper authorities. And since there's a question of ownership, if I were you I'd impound the shirt he's wearing."

She pinned me with a stern look and added, "Along with Mr. Bailey's torn shirt, which my other client, Rose Ann Marstead, is going to give to your chief of security. The Miami police should be able to establish the rightful owners of both shirts and determine whether the pocket that was found came from Mr. Bailey's shirt."

"Done," the captain said.

Glory didn't miss a beat. "For the continued safety of my client, Enrique Urbino, I would suggest that he remain confined under guard until we reach Miami."

"Glory!" I cried out.

"With permission for his three friends to visit him at various times during the day while we are at sea tomorrow."

The captain nodded, then turned to Mr. Jansen with an expression of relief. "While we are in port, you will be confined to the ship," he said, "and will continue your duties until we reach Miami. "As for your further employment with our cruise line—"

"I'm fired," Mr. Jansen said. He looked relieved too.

"That's correct," Captain Olson told him.

As we left the captain's office, Glory put an arm around my shoulders. "You understand why I want Ricky kept under guard," she said. "I'm concerned for his safety. This is a very large ship, and there may be others besides Mr. Bailey and Mr. Jansen who will be tempted to try something."

"I understand," I said, and hugged her. "Thanks for helping Ricky."

"And helping you," she reminded me. "You may find you're in enough trouble with the INS authorities when we arrive back in the United States. Whatever you do, don't get involved in any other scheme concerning Ricky."

I didn't answer Glory. I couldn't promise. Glory couldn't begin to understand that I had to do everything I could to keep Ricky, the one and only love of my life, from being sent back to Cuba.

On our last day at sea, Neil, Julieta, and I faithfully visited Ricky during each half-hour period the captain had allowed us. It wasn't enough time.

Glory and her partner didn't win the bridge tournament, but she didn't seem to care. It was obvious that she was enjoying working as an attorney again. She met twice with Captain Olson and the chief of security. Things were once more happy between us, and she loyally reported to me.

"The captain wants as few passengers as possible to be around when the INS officials arrive to take charge of Ricky," she said. "He's going to start disembarking proceedings immediately upon docking, and once all the passengers have left the ship, he'll allow the INS officers to come aboard."

I couldn't see through my tears. "I want to stay with Ricky as long as possible," I said. "He needs someone to be with him when the officials come."

"Rosie, you know you can't remain on board," Glory said. "You have to leave with the other passengers."

I sighed. "As Ricky's attorney, can you stay with him?"

"Yes," Glory said. "I should be on hand to make sure his arrest is handled properly. I'll wait for the INS in the lounge, but I want you to leave the ship with Eloise and Neil and wait for me in the terminal where our baggage will be collected."

A tear ran down my nose and I rubbed it away. "Ricky can't go back to Cuba," I pleaded with her.

"That will be up to the INS," she answered. "To be honest with you, since Ricky is a minor and he hasn't set foot on U.S. soil, there's a good chance he'll be sent back."

I let out a sob. I couldn't help it.

Glory patted my arm and smiled encouragingly. "On the other hand, if his uncle can manage to stall things in the courts, Ricky will reach his eighteenth birthday in less than two months and will be free of that custodian-guardian control. There'll be plenty of supporters for his cause. I suppose you know that."

"No," I said. "What supporters?"

"Ricky's uncle has a great many friends in the Cuban population of Miami. The captain has been warned that there will be demonstrations at the pier, along with a large number of media people. The Miami police are going to set up barriers to keep them from the pier itself."

"Will the demonstrations and publicity help?"

Glory shrugged. "Who knows?" She hugged me and said, "Don't look so mournful, Rosie. There will be other loves in your life."

"Not like Ricky."

"Remember Rose Calvert in the movie? She had a granddaughter, which means that after she loved and lost Jack, she married and had children."

"But did she love her husband?"

"Maybe even more than she had loved Jack. Life didn't end for her. She had spunk. She kept going."

And so would I, I knew, because there were things I had to do. I had to keep Ricky from being sent back to Cuba. I'd figure out how. I knew I would.

———

On Sunday morning we docked in Miami at eight-thirty, but we had all awakened much earlier and eaten a quick breakfast. Our luggage had been placed outside our doors and collected the night before, so we were left with only our carry-ons.

All passengers had been ordered to report to the

main lounge at eight-thirty sharp, so at eight Neil, Julieta, and I met in the passageway outside Ricky's stateroom. I had on the jeans and T-shirt I planned to wear on the flight home, Julieta was in a pink shorts-and-shirt outfit, and Neil was again wearing his awful long-sleeved nylon shirt with the pink flamingos, his straw hat jammed firmly on his head. He looked like a candidate for the worst-dressed tourist of the month. He looked like a nerd. He looked like Neil. I sighed and squeezed his hand. No matter what his appearance, he was the nicest kind of guy.

Stepping up to the guard at the door, I said, "We've come to say goodbye to Ricky."

"The captain didn't say—" the guard began.

Julieta began to cry. "He's our friend. We'll never see him again. You have to let us see him."

"Just for a few minutes. Please?" I begged.

The guard looked uncomfortable. "I don't have today's orders, but . . ." His forehead puckered, and the corners of his mouth turned down. "Okay," he said. "No more than ten minutes. I'll open the door when you have to leave."

"Okay," Neil said. "Thanks."

We filed into the room, where Ricky was sitting on the edge of one of the twin beds. He was wearing slacks, the cruise line's T-shirt, and his straw hat. "It wouldn't fit in the suitcase," he said when he saw me looking at it.

We all sat with him, and a couple of tears I

couldn't keep back rolled down my cheeks. "I'm going to miss you," I said.

Ricky put his arms around me and said, "Rose, how can I thank you for all—"

Neil interrupted in a gruff voice. "Stop crying, Rose," he said. "We haven't got much time."

He was right. It seemed like only a few minutes before the guard opened the door. "You kids gotta go," he said.

We filed out. "Goodbye, Ricky," Julieta said.

Ricky sat bent over in dejection, his arms resting on his knees, his hat covering his face. He didn't say goodbye, and I didn't trust myself to speak either.

Someone over the loudspeaker advised passengers with blue slips to disembark, collect their luggage, and go through customs.

"Blue slip," Julieta said, holding it up. She gave me a quick goodbye hug and said, "I'll never forget this trip. E-mail me, Rosie. Tell me everything."

"Goodbye, Neil," she said. She ducked under his hat's wide brim to kiss his cheek, and she hugged him longer than she needed to.

"Julieta, hurry up!" her mother called from the doorway. In a moment Julieta had gone.

"Green slip holders may now disembark," the loudspeaker voice said, so we hurried to where Neil's grandmother was parked in her wheelchair with two of the other bridge club members.

I gave a wave to Glory, who was sitting near the

service desk in the lounge waiting for the INS, just as she had promised. I followed Neil and Mrs. Fleming in her wheelchair down the ramp to the terminal where we'd collect our luggage. For a fleeting moment I wondered how attached Neil's grandmother was to his gaudy Hawaiian shirt and straw hat.

I moved in under the wide hat brim. "I'll take over now," I said to Ricky, who was wearing Neil's clothes. The plan had actually worked. "Hurry. I can see a line of taxis right outside the door. Take one to the central Miami police station."

"We may never see each other again, Rose, but I will always remember you and all that you and your friends did to help me," Ricky said. He gave me a quick kiss and was gone.

"Where's Neil going?" Mrs. Fleming asked me.

"Neil will be back soon," I shouted at her. "He's doing a favor for me." In spite of the ache in my throat, I gave a long sigh of relief as I saw Ricky's cab take off, heading into Miami. He had set foot on United States soil. He could ask for political asylum. He could show authorities one of Major Cepeda's flyers to easily prove that his life would be in danger if the INS returned him to Cuba.

"We'll wait over here for Glory and Neil," I told Mrs. Fleming, and I wheeled her chair to a bench against the wall. I sat beside her.

"I knew you and Neil would have a good time together," she said. "He's a fine boy, isn't he?"

She was right. Neil was a fine person. He was bravely sitting alone in the Urbinos' stateroom, waiting for Glory and the INS. "He's a very special guy," I told her. "He'll always be a good friend."

I'd need a good friend. And so would Neil. We'd stand by each other. I didn't know whether Glory would be angry when she discovered Neil waiting for her instead of Ricky. I didn't know how Mr. Wilson or Captain Olson would react. Probably a lot of people would be mad, and Neil and I would be in big trouble.

Neil had said he was willing to take the risk because no one could truly live without freedom. I felt the same way, and I had the feeling that my mother would understand and even be proud.

Ricky was safely in the United States, and that was what mattered most to me. As for what would happen to Neil and me, I wasn't worried. We had a very good attorney.

"It's very tiring sitting here," Mrs. Fleming said. "It was a nice cruise, though. When I get back home, I'm going to take a hot bath and a nice, long nap." She peered into my face. "What are you going to do, Rosie?"

"When we finally get home? Well, first, I'm going to hug my mom, and then I'll call my friend Becca," I said. "I've got so much to tell her."

ABOUT THE AUTHOR

JOAN LOWERY NIXON has been called the grande
dame of young adult mysteries and is the author of
more than a hundred books for young readers, including *Nobody's There; Who Are You?; The Haunt-
ing; Murdered, My Sweet; Don't Scream; Spirit
Seeker; Shadowmaker; Secret, Silent Screams; A
Candidate for Murder; Whispers from the Dead;*
and the middle-grade novel *Search for the Shadow-
man.* Joan Lowery Nixon was the 1997 president of
the Mystery Writers of America and is the only
four-time winner of the Edgar Allan Poe Best Juve-
nile Mystery Award. She received the award for *The
Kidnapping of Christina Lattimore, The Séance,
The Name of the Game Was Murder,* and *The
Other Side of Dark,* which was also a winner of the
California Young Reader Medal. Her historical fic-
tion includes the award-winning series The Orphan
Train Adventures and the Colonial Williamsburg:
Young Americans series.

Joan Lowery Nixon lives in Houston with her
husband.